MAGIC TIDES

Magic Tides

Ebook ISBN: 9781641972512
KDP POD ISBN: 9798372470163
IS POD ISBN: 9781641972529

NYLA Publishing
121 W. 27th St, Suite 1201, NY 10001, New York.
http://www.nyliterary.com

MAGIC TIDES

KATE DANIELS: WILMINGTON YEARS

BOOK 1

ILONA ANDREWS

[1]

Kate

Ms. Vigue adjusted her bright red glasses and peered at me from her perch on the sofa in our second living room. We were in the middle of renovations, and the second living room was one of the four functional rooms in the entire place.

Ms. Vigue was in her early fifties, with lightly tanned skin and ash-blond hair cropped short and brushed back from her face. Her eyes behind the lenses were either gray or pale blue. She wore a silky green blouse with a light gray skirt and looked put together enough to attend a business brunch.

I wore a pair of old shorts and a paint-stained tank top over a sports bra, because I had been painting one of the spare bedrooms when Ms. Vigue arrived unannounced. I'd pulled my brown hair into a bun and pinned it in place with an old bandana to minimize the paint exposure, and since that side of the house had neither fans nor any other way of cooling, I smelled like a lumberjack after a long day at work. Making a great first impression on a school administrator—check.

We smiled at each other. Ms. Vigue was doing her best to

appear approachable, while I did my best to appear harmless. We were both lying as hard as we could.

Making small talk was not among my few virtues. "I was under the impression that we were already done with admissions. You sent us the acceptance letter."

Which was part of the reason we moved here and got stuck in renovation hell.

"You are correct." Ms. Vigue offered me a quick, humorless smile. "Our school is unique."

You could say that again. It was so unique, it cost an arm and a leg. We jumped through two months' worth of hoops and paperwork just for the privilege of an interview, and then spent another month waiting for their decision. They came highly recommended, but I was done with their nonsense.

"We like to think of our student body as being truly representative of the diverse world we live in."

Ms. Vigue slid into her speech mode. It probably worked wonders on trustees and alumni during their fundraising.

"It's a special place where students of different backgrounds come together. This interview will help us to better understand your child's needs and enable us to ensure their safety and help them thrive in our vibrant community."

Aha. This wasn't a get-to-know-you visit. This was a threat assessment. We already went through that during admissions. Why was she yanking our chain again?

I smiled. Curran and I had agreed to maintain a low profile after moving. *Think normal suburban thoughts.* How hard could this be, right? We were just a small family renovating our new home.

"Of course, my husband and I will answer any reasonable questions. Please feel free to ask."

She took out a leather folder, unzipped it, and checked the contents. "You've been recommended by one of our patrons. How do you know Dr. Cole?"

Telling her that Doolittle had patched me up far too many

times to count would just derail the conversation. "He was our family doctor. He delivered Conlan and treated him frequently over the years. We consider him a family friend."

Ms. Vigue nodded and made a note in her folder. "Your son's assessment scores are quite remarkable."

Was this a compliment? If I took it as a compliment, she wouldn't be able to do anything about it. "Thank you."

"Our school's reputation ensures that we get the most outstanding applicants. Your son will be among his intellectual peers."

That would be a tall order, but I didn't need him to find his intellectual equals. I just needed him to learn to act like a person and interact with other children without the weight of his identity dragging him down.

"It's my understanding that your child is a shapeshifter."

Here we go. "Yes."

"What is the nature of his beast?"

I smiled even sweeter. "That's a highly illegal question, Ms. Vigue. The nature of one's beast is confidential and cannot be used as basis for discrimination by any educational institution in this country."

I knew this because my husband had dumped massive amounts of money and effort into lobbying for those laws to be passed before we had met.

Ms. Vigue pushed her glasses up her nose with her middle finger.

Aha. Screw you too. "Would you like me to cite the relevant federal and state statutes protecting shapeshifter rights, or can we skip the formalities?"

"Of course, we cannot compel you to release that information. However..."

"Your next words will determine what I tell Dr. Cole tonight when he calls to check how we are settling in. And he will call. He is very thoughtful and thorough. I'm sure he and his seven thousand associates will take a dim view of your school attempting to discriminate against a shapeshifter child."

Her eyes narrowed. "You're going to be difficult, aren't you?"

You have no idea. "I don't know what you mean, Ms. Vigue. Did you have any other questions?"

"I will come straight to the point."

"I wish you would."

"Can you guarantee that your child will not snap and attack his classmates?"

"Absolutely. He is very much like his father. It's important to him that his resorting to violence is viewed as a deliberate choice rather than a loss of control on his part."

She blinked at me.

No matter how much social outreach shapeshifters did, other humans never forgot that each one of them was a potential spree killer-in-waiting. I had expected better from a person who worked with children.

"Since we've decided to be blunt, if my child decides to go on a rampage, the combined security of your school won't be able to stop him. If something alarming happens, which it won't, you will call us, and either I or his father will come and take care of it."

"Are you suggesting that we make no effort to contain him?"

"Conlan won't attack you if you don't present a threat. Your best strategy is to sit still and look down. Don't run because he will chase you, and he is very fast. Cringing and urinating on yourself will also remove you from his target list."

She blinked again.

"As I said, this is highly unlikely. Your vibrant student body will be perfectly safe. Now I have a question for you. Did the school send you here or did you take it upon yourself to conduct this interview?"

"As Vice Dean of Students..."

Just as I thought. She came on her own. I gave her my pretty smile. Ms. Vigue went silent mid-word.

Normal was overrated anyway.

"I'm so glad we had this chat, Ms. Vigue. Would you like some iced tea for the road?"

Three minutes later, I stood in the doorway to the main building and watched her get into her Chevy Malibu and roll down the road heading west. I took a deep breath and let it out slowly. The air smelled like sea and sun. It should've been calming, but it wasn't.

The past few days brought one minor calamity after another, starting with the floor in the utility room caving in and getting worse from there. Ms. Vigue's visit was just a rotten cherry on top of this cake of woe.

My husband, my son, and I had toured the school, and all three of us liked the teachers and what they were teaching. We had liked the administrative staff for the most part as well. The same couldn't be said about the Office of the Dean of Students. I had met three members of it so far, including Ms. Vigue, and every one of them tried my patience. I wouldn't have had a problem reassuring them if they had made the slightest effort to communicate with us on equal terms.

I needed to vent some steam in the worst way.

My son emerged from behind the wall with an unfamiliar boy in tow. Conlan was large for his age, with my dark hair and his father's gray eyes. The boy next to him was about the same size but probably a year or two older, maybe 9 or 10. Thin, dark haired, with bronze skin and brown eyes, he seemed like he wasn't sure what would happen next. A bit jumpy.

Conlan stopped in front of me. "Hi, Mom. This is Jason. He is Paul's nephew."

Paul Barnhill was our general contractor. Jason gave me a hesitant wave.

"Can we have some sandwiches?" Conlan asked.

When it came to making friends, my son took his cues from

his father. Food first. And he knew where the fridge was and had been making his own sandwiches since he was 2 years old.

"Absolutely."

"Thank you. Jason's brother was kidnapped."

Ah. So, it wasn't about the sandwiches.

Conlan turned to Jason. "Come on."

The two of them went inside. Grendel, our mutant black poodle, trotted out from behind the wall, gave me a lick on the leg in passing, depositing a small army of foul-smelling bacteria on my thigh, and bounded after them.

Food had a particular significance to shapeshifters. They didn't share it with just anyone. Conlan brought Jason to me, made sure I saw Jason's face, made sure that I knew he was about to make him a sandwich, and then informed me that Jason had a problem. A problem I now wanted to know more about, because Jason wasn't some abstract child my son casually knew but someone he accepted and wanted to share a meal with.

"Kidnapped" could mean a lot of things to a 9-year-old boy. The first night after we moved in, a half-naked Conlan informed me that Grendel had been kidnapped by pirates. I grabbed my sword and ran to the shoreline, to find Grendel in a boat tied to a beached tree, floating 5 feet away from shore and barking his head off, while a Jolly Roger my son drew with wall primer on his black T-shirt flew overhead. But we lived in unsafe times. Real kidnappings weren't uncommon, especially if the victim was, in Ms. Vigue's words, "vibrant" enough.

The fort around me vanished, and for a painful second I was sprinting down the street, ice-cold from fear, desperately searching the ruins around me for the spark of baby Conlan's magic and wishing with every fiber of my being that I would find him before his would-be kidnappers did.

I sighed and went to look for Paul.

Finding Paul took a few minutes because our new house was unusually large.

I circled the third stack of lumber in the middle of the courtyard. Around me the walls of Fort Kure loomed against the sunshine, blocking the view of the beach. Local legend said that some harebrained millionaire came to view historic Fort Fisher and was rather underwhelmed, because only a small portion of the original defense installation remained. He conceived Fort Kure as a "companion attraction" to the historic landmark, a sea stronghold on steroids that would give the tourists all the citadel thrills Fort Fisher was missing. For unknown reasons, the millionaire had bailed when the construction was 2/3 complete.

Once finished, Fort Kure would become an ultra-secure dwelling, a hybrid offspring of a medieval castle and a modern citadel. My husband took one look at the absurdly thick stone walls, the tower, and the Atlantic spreading as far as the eye could see and fell in love. His gray eyes had gotten this slightly deranged light, and he had taken my hands in his and said, "Baby, we would be crazy to not do this."

I said yes because I loved him. And because we needed to get out of Atlanta, where everyone knew who we were and what we were capable of. If we stayed there, Conlan would never experience anything resembling a normal childhood. Okay, so "normal" was a stretch, but at least here he would be treated as just another shapeshifter kid, not the son of a former Pack leader, a wonder-child capable of miraculous things. Bottom line, we'd needed a secure base, so we bought Fort Kure at a steep discount and proceeded to sink loads of money into it. The walls were done, so was the front gate, and the rest of the house inside was coming along. Slowly. Very slowly. If everything stayed on schedule, it might be habitable by fall.

I found Paul by the gift shop, which we planned to convert into a stable. He was talking to a man I didn't recognize, and he seemed upset. Paul didn't get upset. He was an optimistic guy who looked at a collapsed wall with an attitude of "I can fix it" and frequently did. The man he was talking to was about ten years older than Paul, which put him in his late forties. They had to be related—both had the same bronze skin, dark curly hair, and aquiline noses.

"...Can't."

"I know," the man said.

"If I give you that money, I can't make payroll. The work's already done. I must run the payroll. I can't ask my people to work for free."

"I know," the man said again. There was a brittle finality to his voice. He had resigned himself to "no" but was too desperate to not try.

Paul dragged his hand through his hair. "Look, I've still got Dad's truck." He dug into his pocket and pulled a keyring out. "I never got around to fixing it. Take it, sell it for parts. It won't bring much, but at least it's something..."

Paul saw me. His mouth clicked shut.

"Hello," I said. "I've met Jason. He says your nephew was kidnapped."

The two men stared at me.

"This is my brother, Thomas," Paul said finally. "Someone took his son. We're trying to scrape together enough money to try to buy him back."

"Do you know who took him?"

"Yes," Thomas said.

I waited. Paul nudged him.

"The Red Horn Nation," Thomas said finally.

"Who are they?"

"A local gang," Paul said. "They control a lot of South Wilmington. Mostly they deal in drugs, but they steal kids too."

"How big are they?"

Paul frowned. "Fifty people? Maybe more."

A nice round number. "Are they holding him for ransom?"

"No," Thomas said.

"Have you tried the cops?"

"These are dangerous people," Thomas said. "The cops won't bother them unless there is evidence. I don't have evidence."

"Then how do you know who took him?"

"There were witnesses."

And if those witnesses went to the police, bad things would happen to them. Right.

"How old is your son, and when did they take him?"

Thomas didn't answer.

"Darin is 16," Paul said. "They took him five days ago. Why is the age important?"

"Because little kids are usually sold to sexual predators or to families who want a child. Teenagers are sold to someone who will keep them confined. Transporting them is risky."

Darin was probably still in the city.

"You were gathering money, so you know where they are," I told Thomas.

He nodded. "They have a house."

"Good." I pulled the rag off my head. "Wait here. I'm going to change, and we'll go and get your son back."

"You don't understand," Thomas said. "They are..."

"Bad people. You've told me."

The Barnhill brothers looked skeptical. It was probably my winning ensemble of stained tank top and torn shorts.

My husband walked out of the north tower and jogged over to us. He was almost six feet tall, with blond hair and gray eyes, and he was built like a champion grappler in his prime. The two men instinctively stepped aside to make room for him.

"Hey."

"Hey," I told him.

"What's going on?"

"Paul's nephew has been kidnapped by a local gang. About 50 people. I'm going to get him back."

Curran grinned at me. "Will you be home in time for dinner?"

Paul and Thomas looked at him like he had lost his mind.

"Naah. Eat without me." I stretched my shoulders a bit, gave him a quick hug, and headed to our bedroom.

"Red Horn kills people," Thomas said behind my back. "Your wife…"

"Will enjoy the exercise," my husband said. "You know what they say. Happy wife, happy life."

Five minutes later I walked out wearing my work clothes: a pair of jeans loose enough to kick someone taller than me in the face, a gray T-shirt, and a pair of soft boots. I wore a utility belt on my waist and a sword sheath on my back. The handle of my sword protruded over my shoulder. I'd braided my hair, and there were two throwing knives and a Bowie in the sheath on my thigh.

I gave Curran a quick hug.

"Don't forget," he said.

"Low profile. I remember." I turned to Thomas. "Let's go."

Thomas looked at his brother. Paul spread his arms and shrugged. Thomas looked at him, looked at me, and fell in step.

"Did you bring a car?"

"I rode a horse."

"Good. I like horses best." They always worked.

The world skipped a beat. Technology coughed and died, and magic flooded us in an invisible wave. Colors grew a little brighter, sounds became a little louder, and things came into sharper focus. For as long as the magic held, guns would not fire, electric bulbs would remain dark, and monsters would spawn in the darkness. I looked up at the horizon.

"I still think this is a terrible idea, Mrs…"

"Don't worry," I told him. "Like Curran said, I need the exercise. And, please, call me Kate."

As I watched my wife ride away, I knew our life of quiet anonymity here was over. Despite her promises to the contrary, whatever she did would be loud and messy. It was time to find my son.

"What do you think she's going to do?" Paul asked.

"She will find the hornet's nest and set it on fire. When the angry hornets fly out, she'll poke them with her sword."

"You don't seem that worried," Paul said.

"I'm not. She's almost as good as she thinks she is. Don't tell her I said that. Seriously."

We watched Kate and Thomas riding away some more.

"Why Red Horn?" I asked.

"Who knows?" Paul shrugged. "Mess with the bull, get the horns? They are a vicious bunch, I can tell you that."

They'd have to be to steal a child.

"Okay. Umm," he hesitated.

"What is it?"

"My family, we don't have a lot of money..."

I waited and said nothing.

"I can give you a good deal on the renovation, maybe."

"No need. We've already agreed on a fair price for this." I waved my arm to indicate my fortress in progress. "That's settled."

"Well, is there anything we can do?"

I locked eyes with him and put a little bit of weight into my stare.

"Yes. You can go and get your family and bring them here. Paul, listen carefully. When I say family, I mean everybody. Your family. Thomas' family. Close friends, people you care about. People who could be hurt or threatened to get at you. Do you understand?"

He almost staggered back. I may have overdone it a bit, but this was important.

"Yes. I can do that."

"Good. Go and do it now. I'll keep Jason here. He can help my son and I prepare."

"For what?" he asked.

"A siege."

"A what?"

"Paul, we don't have a lot of time. Kate is going to do what she does. She's going to ask some very dangerous people some very pointed questions about who took your nephew and why. People will get hurt; some may die. Their friends will want revenge. They will look for her. And you. And your family. If you and yours are here, I can keep everybody safe. Please go and get them. Now."

He left without any more questions. Now I needed to find Conlan. We had a lot of work to do, and I needed to explain some things.

The wind was blowing in from the sea. I followed his scent to a rope tied to a beached tree on the shore. At the other end of the rope, about forty feet out, was a "boat" my son had found and repaired.

Grendel turned at my approach, saw my face, and lay down in the boat with only his eyes visible. Grendel was a smarter-than-average dog.

The boys' backs were turned to me, as they were staring out to sea and the adventures that waited there. I pulled the rope. Hard.

The boat rocketed back to land.

Conlan hit the sand before it did, landing in a crouch.

"Wow," Jason exclaimed. "Your dad is strong!"

"And quiet," Conlan said. "I didn't know you were there."

"I didn't want you to know. We can talk while you clear the lumber in front of the fort."

"Are you in trouble? I didn't want to get you in trouble." Jason turned to me. "I can go home, Mr. Lennart."

I didn't believe in lying to children.

"Nobody is in trouble, Jason. You're staying here. My wife is going to find your brother. The people who took him won't like it, and they'll come back here tonight looking to even the score."

A golden light rolled over Conlan's irises.

"Yes, we'll get to that," I told him. "But if we're having guests, even uninvited ones, we need to tidy up the place. The space in front of the wall is a mess."

"We're cleaning up for the bad people?" Jason asked.

Jason was young and had been through a lot recently, so I couldn't blame him if he was having trouble keeping up. That was okay—my son understood me just fine.

"He means that there are plenty of places for the bad people to hide behind. He wants to see them sneaking up on us."

Understanding dawned on Jason's face. "My family..."

"Will be safe behind the walls. Your father is fetching them back here. Everything will be alright. Meanwhile, you can help us get ready."

[2]

Kate

When humans had prophesized about the Apocalypse, we had always expected it would be fast. Oh, there would be war and natural disasters and other preliminaries that might take their time, but the actual moment when the world ended would be swift. A rain of fire, a nuclear mushroom cloud, a meteor, a catastrophic volcanic eruption... And when magic hit us for the first time, it had delivered exactly what we anticipated.

Planes fell out of the sky. Electricity shorted out. Guns stopped working. Ordinary, normal humans turned into monsters or started shooting lightning from their fingertips. Ravenous mythical creatures spawned out of thin air. For three days the magic had raged, and then it vanished, leaving a mountain of casualties in its wake. Just as the world reeled and tried to pick up the pieces, the magic came again, and the slow crawl of the Apocalypse began.

We called that first magical tsunami the Shift, and everything after post-Shift. Magic flooded our world in waves, without warning, smothering technology, gradually chewing skyscrapers into dust, and slowly but surely changing the very fabric of our existence. Landscape, climate, flora, fauna, people—nothing was left untouched. Nobody could predict how long the waves lasted or how intense they would be. Over the past half a century, we learned to live with it.

Wilmington had fared better than most cities. Certainly, better than Atlanta where we came from. For one, it was a century and change older. Being older helped. And it wasn't nearly as built up as Atlanta, where the once-glistening office towers and high-rises lay in ruins. Magic had taken a solid bite out of the city but didn't quite reduce it to rubble.

Wilmington hadn't escaped unscathed. Some of the taller buildings had fallen. The Cape Fear Memorial Bridge was no more. It had collapsed in that first magic wave. The Murchison Building had slowly turned to dust until it finally imploded. The spire of the First Baptist Church, once the tallest point of the city, had broken off one day and crashed onto the street, killing several people. But the main damage had been done by floods.

The sea level had risen, partially due to pre-Shift global warming and partially due to magic issues nobody fully understood. Now parts of the city looked like Venice with bridges, sometimes solid, sometimes cobbled together with whatever was handy at the time, spawning canals, ponds, and marshes.

Thomas and I rode across one of those bridges now, the hoofbeats of our mounts thudding on the worn wood. He rode an old bay mare. I rode Cuddles. When Thomas first saw Cuddles, he gave her a side-eye. She stood ten feet tall, including the two-foot ears, and was splattered with random spots of black and white. She was also a donkey, a mammoth jenny, to be exact.

Horses had their advantages, but most of them spooked easily. I once rode Cuddles across a rickety bridge infested with magical snakes, and she stomped right over the hissing serpents like they weren't even there and then pranced when we reached the solid ground.

Unfortunately, Cuddles failed to reassure Thomas of my badassness. Getting information out of him was like pulling teeth. He didn't trust me at all, and as he rode next to me, his entire body communicated that he thought coming on this adventure with me was a very bad idea.

I'd met Thomas' type before. He kept things in. In the chaos of the magic and tech mad dance, Thomas was a calm rock on which his family could always rely. He handled his problems on his own, without any fanfare. Except now his son was taken, and he couldn't solve this problem on his own. A lot of people would be frantic, with their emotions spilling over, but Thomas went even deeper inward, all the way down. He was a hair above catatonic. Sooner or later, he would explode. It would be better if that happened sooner, before we got to where we were going.

I had run across all sorts of human scum, but traffickers were at the very top of my shit list.

"How did it happen?"

"They came in a car and took him off the street," Thomas said.

"What was he doing at the time?"

"He was playing soccer with his friends."

"And they only took him? Not any of his friends?"

Thomas nodded.

This smelled like a targeted grab.

"Is Darin special in any way?"

"No."

"Does he have any enemies?"

"No."

"Is he handsome? Is anybody obsessed with him?"

"No."

"Does he have any magic?"

There was a small pause before Thomas answered. "No."

Right. We would have to work on the trust bit.

"Have you tried the Order?" I asked.

Thomas sighed.

The Order of Merciful Aid was a knight order that functioned as a private law enforcement organization. They took petitions from the public and charged on a sliding scale. Their services were reasonable. Their definition of "aid," not so much. Their definition of "human" was also rather narrow.

"We have a small chapter in Wilmington," Thomas said. "There are only three knights. They are busy."

True, but the kidnapping of a child would be a priority even for the overworked knights. There was something about Darin that Thomas wanted to keep hidden. Pushing him about it would get me nowhere.

That was fine. The day was still young.

"What kind of person is Darin?"

Thomas turned and looked at me as if I'd punched him.

"What sort of kid is he?" I asked.

"You want to know what kind of person my son is? I'll tell you. Jason has a friend who comes down here during the summer to visit his grandma and grandpa. Last summer they went down to the beach after a storm. Jason told him not to go into the water, but the boy thought he was a good swimmer and the boy's grandfather said it was fine as long as they didn't go out too far."

That did not sound good.

"The boy got caught by a riptide, and it pulled him out into the ocean. Jason ran to get Darin and by the time they made it back to the beach, you couldn't even see him anymore. Nothing but ocean. Darin went in after him. Somehow, he found the boy. They washed up three miles down the shore in the marsh, and then Darin carried that exhausted child all the way home through the marsh filled with leeches and God knows what. That's the kind of person my son is."

Thomas looked me straight in the eye. "But even if he was a lazy, terrible kid, I would still be out here, looking for him, because he is my son. My child. I don't know why you're doing this. Maybe it's a power trip for you, maybe you can actually help.

But if you can't, don't waste my time. Don't waste my son's time, because I don't know how much he has left."

Curran

MY EIGHT-YEAR-OLD SON HOISTED AN ENTIRE PALLET OF LUMBER with a look that asked if it was enough.

Beside him, Jason looked slightly shocked. He was gamely struggling with smaller individual boards.

"Yes, very impressive. Carry it inside the big gate and then meet out here by the doors. Jason, you're doing fine. I'm just going to borrow Conlan for a minute."

Conlan deposited his burden, trotted back, and stood a respectful distance from me. Waiting. He was my son, but he was also a shapeshifter standing before his alpha.

"Well?"

"Jason is my friend, and his brother was taken. Right off the street. Nobody will help them. Everybody is afraid of those guys."

"Did you ask your mother to find him?"

He hesitated. "Not exactly."

"No. But you knew if you brought Jason to her and mentioned it, she would drop what she was doing and go fix it."

"Yes."

"You manipulated her. I wonder where you learned that?"

Conlan's face turned slightly defiant. "He likes you. He says you're powerful."

"I'm sure he does. Your grandfather says a lot of things."

"He's very old. He knows about a lot of things. He was a king."

"He was that."

"He wanted Mom to be a queen, to rule with him."

No, he didn't. "Do you think he means it?"

Conlan seemed to think it over. "No. He wouldn't share his power. Ever. With anyone."

"Good. That's the most important thing to understand about him."

He frowned. "What does that mean?"

"Your grandfather will never sacrifice anything for your sake. Your mother is his only living child. All the rest, and there were many, are long dead."

"He says he loved them all."

"I'm sure he did in his way. At least until he didn't anymore. Then, he destroyed them."

"Except for Mom."

"Not for a lack of trying," I told him. "Your mom is not like the others. She survived, and she beat him."

"Is she stronger? Is that why she beat him?"

"Your mother is very strong, but that's not why she won. She beat him because she's not like him. He didn't raise her. As young as you are, you've spent more time with him than she ever did."

He squinted at me. "That's what this is about? You don't like me visiting him."

"Yes and no. No, I don't like it, but I don't have to. He's your grandfather. His blood runs through your veins. I can't change that. Learn from him, listen to his stories, but don't ever buy into his bullshit."

"Dad!"

"Have I ever forbidden you to see him?"

"No, but..."

Roland was a wound that wouldn't heal. Trying to keep Conlan away from him would only backfire. The last thing we needed was for our son to discover his magical grandfather when he was 25, because then Roland would be a forbidden secret we had hidden from him. No, we let him visit, and when he came back spouting dangerous nonsense, we dealt with it right then and there. As I was about to do now.

"Yes, Conlan, he was great. An immortal god king who wanted to rule everyone, everywhere and give them all a better life as long as it was on his terms and his alone. Look where that got him. Next time you see him, when he tells you how special you are and how much he loves you, and I know he means every word, really think about where he is now and how he got there. That's all I ask."

"I will. But you were like him."

"How?"

"You were the Beast Lord. You were in charge of everyone like us. You were a king."

"No, I was a pack leader."

Conlan's eyes flashed gold again. "How is that different? People did what you told them to do."

"I also had to do things I didn't want to do. I was responsible for other people's lives and safety. When they died, it was on me. I never wanted the power or the burden of it. Look at Jason."

A couple dozen yards away Jason dropped a board, struggled to pick it up, and finally ended up dragging it toward the gates.

"How good a fighter is he?"

Conlan opened his mouth, looked at Jason, and closed it again.

"Tonight, his family will come here. They are all ordinary humans like him. They don't have our speed, our strength, or our regeneration. People, regular people, are fragile. The most important thing tonight won't be hurting the bad guys. It will be keeping the bad guys from hurting the people under our protection. If we aren't careful, Jason may die tonight."

My son took a step back. "I'll protect Jason! I'll protect all of them."

"There are times when no matter how powerful you are, you aren't enough. You can't be everywhere at once. You have to assume that people will die because of your orders and actions and accept responsibility for it. This is what being a leader means. Your grandfather was too weak to carry that burden. This is how he started on the path that made him an abomination, a man who murdered his children, betrayed his sister, turned your uncle into a butcher, and destroyed the people he was supposed to lead and serve. He had also wanted to protect everyone, and when he couldn't, it broke him."

Conlan stared at me.

I gave him the alpha stare until he lowered his gaze.

"Do you think your mother doesn't know that you manipulated her?"

"She knows," he said quietly. Guilt in his voice. Good.

"She loves you very much, Conlan. Don't abuse that."

"Yes, sir."

"Next time when you need help, you will state your request clearly and honestly. In a very short time, some very bad people will be coming here to harm Jason and his family. And us. I will tell you where to stand and what to do, and you will stand where I told you and do it until I tell you to stop. Do you understand?"

He answered with his eyes still glued to ground, "I understand."

"Good, son. Get to work."

Kate

The Red Horn Nation had their HQ in Lincoln Forest. The first few magic waves had reduced the population at a catastrophic rate, and the survivors quickly figured out that the old rule of safety in numbers still applied. Like many cities, Wilmington had fractured into dense clumps, with neighborhoods bundling together and fortifying, and Lincoln Forest sat right in the middle of everything, near Midtown.

It was a lower-middle-class neighborhood, with brick ranch houses set back on large lots. The surrounding neighborhoods of

Forest Hills cushioned it from every side, so Lincoln Forest didn't bother with a communal defensive wall, leaving fortifications to individual homeowners.

I surveyed the large ranch house. It sat a good distance from the street at the end of a longish driveway. Magic hated high tech buildings, but it loved trees, and the two oaks flanking the driveway looked like they had been growing there for half a millennium, their massive crowns spreading all the way over the street. Three cars waited by the garage, a black Ford truck and a couple of sedans with bloated hoods, modified to run during the magic waves. Modifications like that were expensive. The stolen kid trade must've been profitable.

No defenses, except for the usual bars on the windows and a solid door. No wards that I could feel. Nothing out of the ordinary except for a cow's horn, dipped in bright red paint and stuck onto a metal stick by the driveway, announcing the house's ownership.

"Why Red Horn? Why not Red Blade or something like that?"

"I don't know," Thomas said.

I dismounted. There was no need to tie Cuddles. She wouldn't go anywhere.

"I know that you think you are tough," Thomas said. "But these people, they are violent. Very violent."

"Do you have a picture of Darin with you?"

He reached into his wallet and pulled out a large folded missing poster. On it a lean, dark-haired teenager smiled into the camera. He looked a bit like Thomas and a lot like an older version of Jason.

"Hold on to that."

"They are going to kill you. They've killed people before who came looking for their kids."

"Let's try not to get killed then. I'm going to knock on their door. You can come with, or you can wait here."

Thomas dismounted and tied his horse to the mailbox post.

His face told me that he really didn't want me to go in there. He looked around, went to the nearest oak, where someone had sawed a branch off and left it in pieces, picked up a good size chunk, and looked at me.

"All set?"

He nodded.

I walked up the driveway. On the door, someone had written *RHN* in blood. So good of them to identify themselves. I'd hate to get the wrong house.

I tapped the door with my foot.

It swung open, and a beefy guy in his twenties with ruddy skin and a skull tattoo on his neck peered at me.

"What the fuck do you want?"

"To come inside."

"No."

Most people aimed for the head when they punched. Unfortunately, heads were hard, because our brain was precious, and we'd evolved durable skulls to protect it. I punched him in the solar plexus. He was beefy but not fat, so he didn't have much padding, and since he was a head taller than me, the solar plexus presented a convenient target.

Whatever the guy was expecting, my left uppercut wasn't it. I punched him very fast and very hard. I could remember not being able to read, but I knew how to punch even in my earliest memories. I had over 3 decades of practice.

The gang's doorman folded to the ground. I kicked him in the head to make sure he stayed down there, stepped over his body, and walked inside. Thomas took half a second to come to terms with the body on the ground and followed me brandishing his log.

The house opened into a long rectangular living room that stretched to my left. Directly in front of me a doorway led into the kitchen. There must've been a hallway here at some point, separating the entry hallway from the living room, but the house had been remodeled, and some of the walls had been taken down for a more open floor plan. On my right was another door, which remained closed.

In the living room, two men and a woman lounged on the couches. The coffee table in front of them held a cleaver falchion, which was basically a machete with a cross guard, a mace, and a shotgun. Behind them, at the far wall, four large cages waited, stacked 2 x 2. The cage on the right in the bottom row was full. A little boy with dark hair and a tear-stricken pale face huddled in it, curled into a ball.

If Julie were here with me, I wouldn't have had to lift a finger. She'd been a street kid before she became my ward. The sight of that child in the cage would have been enough to send my kid into a tailspin, and when she came out of it, everyone in this house would be dead.

The three gang members stared at me. One was tall and lean, in his forties, with dish-water blond hair, stubble, and a lantern jaw. His left index finger and pinkie were cut off at the middle phalanges. The other was shorter, stockier, and younger, with olive skin, dark hair cropped down to almost nothing, and a patchwork of tattoos across his neck and arms exposed by a sleeveless black T-shirt. The woman was in her mid-twenties, with a round face, pasty makeup, and light blond hair worn long. Soft, like she didn't swing a weapon for a living. Stylized flame tattoos ran from her wrists up her forearms. Probably a firebug, a fire mage.

A decade ago, I'd quip something funny about borrowing a cup of sugar right about now, but being a parent and having had my child threatened had given me a new perspective. Everyone knew that human trafficking was one of the ugliest lows a human being could sink to. But it was one thing to intellectually understand. It was entirely another thing to have your child taken and stare his kidnapper in the eyes as he cut your son's face.

"The poster," I told Thomas.

He held it up.

"Who did you sell him to?" I asked.

"The fuck..." The shorter man started.

Lantern-jaw man stood up and grabbed the mace off the table. "Jace!"

A door swung open deeper in the house. A moment later a man in his late thirties came out of the kitchen. Jace was broad in the shoulder, dark-haired, tan, and scarred on both cheeks. A short black goatee perched on his chin like a smear of dark hair. He looked like he'd been through a lot of fights and liked putting his hands on people.

Another man followed him, looming a full head above his boss. This one was in his twenties, sun-burned, tall, and sheathed in hard fat. The bruiser.

"I see we got ourselves a mercenary, boys and girls," Jace declared. He'd stopped just outside where he thought my striking distance was. Should have stopped two steps earlier.

"You know what your problem is, Tom?" Jace drawled. "You're too fucking dumb to know when to quit."

The woman on the couch smiled. The other two men by her watched me. The shorter one had relaxed when Jace showed up, but the older blond was still uneasy. You didn't survive into your forties in his line of work without getting a feel for people, and he didn't like what his gut was telling him about me.

Jace kept on. "You should've quit when Dewane here nailed your missing poster to your front door."

Judging by the proud look on the large guy's face, he was the Dewane in question. Thomas had neglected to mention the poster incident. No matter.

"Instead, you hired yourself some broad who's dumb enough to take your money." He turned to me. "Let me tell you how this will go, sweet thing. I'm going to fuck you up and then I'm going to hang—"

I stepped forward and kicked him in the head. I hadn't put my hands up, and he never saw it coming. My foot connected with a meaty smack. Jace's head snapped back. He stumbled and fell flat on his back. Timber.

I pointed to the poster. "Who did you sell him to?"

The slow hamster wheel that powered up Dewane's brain finally processed the fact that his boss was on the floor, groaning. Dewane understood violence. He knew that when violence happened, it was his time to shine. He charged me.

I stepped out of the way. He tore past me, spun around, and I smashed my palm against his right ear. Dewane swayed. Most people would've gone down, but he stayed on his feet, unsteady but upright, and tried to grab me. I leaned back and drove an oblique kick to his knee. The knee collapsed inward with a crunch. Dewane howled and toppled over like a felled tree.

At the couch, the firebug jumped up, her hands rising.

I grabbed the log out of Thomas' hands and threw it at her. It hit her in the chest. She yelped and went down.

Jace rolled to his feet, his face bloody, grabbed the falchion off the table, and came at me. In the half a second he took to cover the distance between us and draw his sword back for a strike, I pulled Sarrat out of its sheath on my back and slashed across his neck. It was a textbook cut, slicing diagonally from below the left ear. The saber's blade severed muscle and the spinal cord with the slightest of resistance. Blood gushed from the cut. His head fell from his shoulders.

The headless body teetered and crashed to the floor.

Everything stopped. The firebug, who'd scrambled up, froze with her hands halfway up. Even Dewane forgot to moan about his ruined knee.

I picked up Jace's head by his hair and held it in front of the poster. "Who did you sell him to?"

The traffickers gaped at me.

I looked back at them. "He can't answer me, but one of you can. I'll go through you one by one, and I'll kill the last of you very slowly. You won't die until you tell me what I want to know. Don't be last."

"Onyx," Lantern Jaw said. "He's a necromancer with the People."

Damn it all to hell. Talking to the People was the last thing I wanted.

"Was this a random grab or a special order?"

"A special order," he said. "He asked for the kid by name. I don't know why. Jace didn't ask."

I dropped the head. "Good."

The firebug glared at me. Her hands twitched.

I pinned her down with my stare. "Try me."

The woman looked into my eyes. All the fight went out of her. She swallowed and shook her head.

A wise decision, but she gave up kind of quick.

"This is done." I indicated the house around us with Sarrat's point. "This criminal enterprise is finished. Your gang is finished. If I see you again, I'll kill you. Leave here, take nothing." I pointed at the firebug. "You stay."

The shorter trafficker looked at Lantern Jaw. "Are we just …"

"Yeah." Lantern Jaw skirted around Jace's body and headed to the door.

"What about Dewane?" the shorter guy said.

"Fuck Dewane." Lantern Jaw went out the door.

The shorter guy blinked, thought about it, then grabbed Dewane's arm, strained, and got him upright. They struggled past me. At the doorway, the shorter man bared his teeth at me.

"This isn't fucking over. We'll come for you."

"Fort Kure, on the beach. You can't miss it. Get the whole gang, get your friends, their friends, and people they know. Bring everybody. Save us all some time."

They staggered outside.

I went to the cage with the little boy. It was locked with a simple padlock. I looked at the firebug. She grabbed the lock. Her fingers shook so it took her three tries to get it open. I took the little boy out of the cage. He was so thin, he weighed almost nothing. His fingers were bruised and there was a burn on his right forearm, where someone had put out a cigarette. He stared at me with big, dark eyes. I hugged him gently, and he clung to me, as if afraid I would disappear.

"Are there more?"

The firebug nodded.

THERE WERE THREE MORE IN CAGES IN THE BASEMENT. TWO BOYS and a girl, none over the age of six. The girl and the oldest boy knew their addresses, the two younger kids only knew their first and last names, but it was enough to go on.

We put two boys onto Thomas' horse. I settled the little girl on to Cuddles and lifted the smallest boy into the saddle in front of her.

"Hold on to him, kiddo."

She nodded. She was short and dark-haired, with round cheeks and dark brown eyes, but something about her reminded me of Julie. Maybe it was the way she hugged the little boy. Like she had decided that this was her job and was determined to do it.

The firebug waited for me on the lawn. I surveyed the house and the three vehicles in the driveway. "Torch it."

She did a doubletake. "There are money and weapons in there..."

"I know."

She raised her hands. Magic swirled inside her, slow and sluggish. Moments crawled by. Her power was moving now, a ghostly outline of a pinwheel of flames forming between her fingers. She strained, spinning it more and more tightly with her hands, winding it into an invisible ball until it glowed with nearly white light. She held it there for as long as she could, trying to build it up, but it broke free. The fireball ignited to life, streaked to the house, and smashed into the front window.

Thunder pealed, the sound of magic bursting from containment of the spell. Glass exploded, and flames surged in the living room.

The firebug waved her arms around. Now her earlier hesitation made sense. She needed a lot of time to get her power going, while I only needed a fraction of a second to swing my sword.

Twin flame jets erupted from the woman's hands and washed over the house and the cars.

Pre-Shift, this would have gone down completely differently. There would have been a formal investigation and warrants issued by the court. There would be due process, a trial, and public outrage. Now it was just me.

It wasn't that cops were inept or corrupt. It was that they were stretched thin, and the power difference between them and the magically juiced-up criminals was often too vast. We lived in an unsafe age where one individual could overpower thousands if their magic was strong enough. My father was the living example of how that setup could go catastrophically wrong. Given a choice, I would take the pre-Shift system over ours any day.

The house was fully engulfed now, and the firebug was breathing hard and sweating.

"Stay here until it burns itself out."

"You're letting me go?" she asked.

I nodded. "If I find out that this neighborhood burned down because you took off, I'll find you."

I started down the street, leading Cuddles on. Thomas gave the firebug the kind of look that would haunt one's nightmares and followed me, guiding his horse. We rounded the corner. Thomas drew even with me. The line of his mouth was straight and hard, like he was trying to keep his words in.

"Share," I told him. "Don't keep me in suspense."

"They are traffickers. Slavers."

"Yes."

"You could've killed them all."

"Yes."

"Why didn't you? They sold Darin. God alone knows what's happening to my son. Do you know how many kids they stole?"

"Many." The cages were grimy and worn, likely used for years.

"Why did you let them go?"

"Your brother said Red Horn Nation has about 50 members."

"Yes."

"What's the most important thing to a gang after money?"

He gave me a blank look.

"Reputation," I said. "Street cred. They run on fear and pride. If I killed them all, it might take them awhile to figure out who did it. If I only left one alive, the rest might not believe what happened. They would want to verify and probably shut that survivor up to buy themselves time to think things over and plan their response. I don't want them to think. I want them to react. "

Thomas blinked at me.

"Very shortly, five people will be explaining to the Red Horn's big boss that I came into their house and squished them like the cockroaches they are. I killed their underboss, slapped them around, made them give up the name of their client, took their merchandise, and set their house on fire. Five people is too many to shut up. They will be making a lot of noise, so if the Red Horn wants to hold on to the tattered shreds of its reputation, they're going to retaliate and fast, before this news spreads. I told them exactly where to find me. They will get every warm body they have down to Fort Kure tonight."

"You want them to attack you?"

"I want them to attack my husband specifically, but yes."

"You're talking about 50 people! Maybe more than 50!"

"Well, they are one less since Jace is dead, so I softened them up for him."

He stared. I winked at him. If the Red Horn thought I was scary, I couldn't wait for them to meet Curran.

"You're crazy," he said.

"When my oldest kid was thirteen, her best friend sold her out to a group of sea demons. The demons tied her to a cross, and she watched as they devoured her birth mother's corpse. When my son was a little over a year old, someone sent a group of assassins to kidnap him. They wanted to eat him so they could grow their power."

Thomas was clearly having a rough time coming to terms with the words coming out of my mouth.

"Of all the human filth, I hate human traffickers the most. Wilmington is too small for both of us. It's either Red Horn or me, and I just finished painting my second living room. I'm not leaving. Do you know how hard it is to make a straight edge along the trim? They used to have painter's tape just for that pre-Shift."

Actually, painting the trim wasn't hard, since I had good hand-eye coordination, but Thomas looked like he needed a bit of humor to nudge him back to reality.

Thomas shook his head, as if waking up. "Where are we going?"

"To the Order." I had a general idea where it was, but Thomas would know for sure.

"Why?"

"Because time is short. We need to drop off the children with someone who can protect them and take them home, while we get over to the People's compound."

Onyx was likely a Master of the Dead or a journeyman. Probably the latter. Masters of the Dead were premier navigators who made too much money and were under too much scrutiny from their power-hungry peers to dabble in human trafficking. But journeymen earned considerably less, and they lived in the dorms, on-base. Onyx had no means of keeping Darin for himself, so he was likely a middleman, an intermediary between the Red Horn Nation and the final buyer.

I seriously doubted that Red Horn people would let Onyx know that I was coming. They had bigger worries right now. Even if they had, he would stay put. He was at his safest in the middle of the People's base. But I didn't want him to warn whoever put in the custom order for Darin.

"Are you going to tell me what's special about your son or do we have to play the guessing game?" I asked.

"He has gills," Thomas said quietly. "He can't drown."

Ah. "Does he transform?"

He nodded.

"Is that something that runs in the family?"

"No. He's the only one."

There was a connection between the population and the mythical creatures spawning. If the area had a lot of Irish settlers, you would get kelpies and selkies. If there was a sizeable Brazilian population, the water might manifest an Iara. Some creatures were harmless, but most weren't, because humans tended to focus on things that could kill and eat them and immortalize them through legends as a warning to future generations. Magic brought those legends back to life, and the more people worried about something, the greater the chance of it manifesting.

Wilmington had a thriving port, which was the reason the city became one of the vital trade centers after the Shift. Shipping by land had become more perilous, and the importance of ports skyrocketed. Not only was the city multicultural, but also crews from just about every part of the world traveled here to unload their cargo, bringing their myths with them. Oceans were deep, and sailors had a healthy respect for them. They believed in aquatic monsters, no matter their mythological origin. It was pointless to try to guess what Darin had turned into. I'd know more when I found him.

"I know you're worried about your family," I said. "My

husband knows me. He would've anticipated what happened and made sure that your and Paul's loved ones are safe. By now they're probably all at the fort."

"The fort that will be attacked?"

"It's the safest place for them. Trust me on this. I need your help finding the Order and then the People, because you know the city better than I do. If you can get me to the Farm, I'll take it from there, and you can join your family."

"Okay," Thomas said.

[3]

"...My second brother, Kody, but we call him Copper, because his hair is red, but Mommy says that all of her brothers had red hair, but it turned blond when they got to be grownups, so Copper is going to be blond for sure..."

The little girl's name was Nika.

"...And my oldest brother, Rylee, has a German Shepherd puppy, and the puppy is named Kenobi, and his paws are this big, and he's going to be a big dog for sure..."

There'd been no warning. We'd been walking for about 10 minutes when Nika took a deep breath and suddenly all the words came out. She hadn't stopped talking for the better part of the hour. Something must've convinced her that we were okay, and she was safe, and all the fear and anxiety she'd held in since the Red Horn snatched her off the street was pouring out of her like a geyser.

"...And Kenobi will be a good protecting dog, because Kenobi is a Jedi name..."

They had played the whole series in a drive-in theater during a tech wave, and Nika's family went to see it. We'd gone to see it too, although their sword fighting made me squeeze my eyes shut a few times.

"For sure?" I asked.

"For sure for sure."

Once she started talking, the other kids had thawed little by little and were now listening.

"I have a dog," the oldest boy said. His name was Caiden and he'd insisted that he knew how to ride so Thomas let him have the reins. I kept an eye on him to make sure I had time to lunge for the horse if it got spooked.

"What's your dog's name?" I asked.

"Yeti."

"What kind of dog is he?" Nika asked.

"He's big and white and he has lots of fur…"

The Wilmington chapter of the Order occupied a historic firehouse on the corner of Castle and 5th Avenue, downtown. A handsome two-story brick building, it had a tomato-red door, white trim, and four-story bell tower. Over the years, the bell had gone from useful to decorative and back to useful again. In an age where a magic wave could take out phones any second, the ability to sound the alarm without electricity was priceless.

The knights had made a few modifications, including grates on the huge downstairs windows. The pale metal bars fluoresced slightly if you squinted at them just right. Steel core plated with a thick layer of silver. Nice.

"…And Copper said that he should have a puppy too, and Daddy said…"

Thomas and I took the children off the horses.

Going to the Order hadn't been the plan, but I had four severely traumatized children on my hands. *Get in, get out, don't mouth off, don't lose your temper. Low profile.* I knocked on the door.

"Come in!" a female voice called.

We did.

The inside of the former firehouse was clean and bright. A single room took up most of the downstairs. The walls were brick, the floor concrete sealed with white. Three desks waited, two in a row on the left, and one on the right. Bookshelves lined the walls, some holding books, the others offering a variety of ingredients, and on the left a metal rack held assorted weapons. There would be more in the armory, somewhere deeper in the building.

The two desks on the left stood empty. A woman in her fifties sat at the one on the right. She looked strong, not just muscular but solid, with a round face, sharp dark eyes, russet-brown skin, and black, curly hair, cut short and streaked lightly with gray. Claudia Ozburn, Knight-Protector and the head of this Order chapter. Curran and I had done a basic background check on who was who in Wilmington, so I knew her by reputation. She was dangerous, smart, and had, reportedly, very little tolerance for nonsense.

Claudia looked at the children, then back at me and raised her eyebrows. The kids went silent.

"We found some missing children," I told her. "I'd like to petition the Order to return them to their parents."

"Where did you find them?"

"In the Red Horn's human kennel."

Claudia's expression didn't change. She reached into the desk drawer on her right, took out a piece of paper, and pushed it across the desk to me. "Fill this out."

Form J-7, unaccompanied minor. In my brief stint with the Order, I had processed so many of those, I could do them in my sleep.

Claudia turned to the children. "You are now under protection of the Order of Merciful Aid. You are safe. We will take good care of you and make every effort to get you back to your parents."

I went through the form, ticking the right boxes on autopilot, put "Kate" in the contact field with my phone number, listed the children's names and descriptions, signed, dated, and slid the form back to her. I could've had Thomas do it, but it would've taken a lot longer. Thomas didn't look like the type to bust down gang doors. She would've kept him for questioning. This was faster.

"You've done this before," she said.

"On occasion."

She studied the form. "Kate with no last name. Are you a merc?"

"Used to be."

"Guilded?"

"Yes."

"Which city?"

I really didn't want to give her any more information than I had to. "Atlanta. Thank you for your assistance, Knight-Protector."

"When I call Atlanta's chapter, what are they going to tell me about you?"

She would call. I could tell by her expression. Claudia had a nickname in the Order. They called her the Badger because she was stubborn like one and once she got a hold of something, she wouldn't let go.

"When you call, ask for Nick Feldman. Tell him Kate brought some kids in. He will vouch for me."

Nick and I had our differences. He was almost a stepbrother, and Conlan called him uncle. He still thought that I was an abomination, but he and I talked before we left for Wilmington. He understood my reasons for leaving and laying low. He wouldn't stab me in the back.

"Okay, Kate. Where are the two of you going from here?"

None of your business.

"To the Farm!" Nika piped up. "Where the undead things are! They are going to save Thomas' son. He's been kidnapped."

Oy. When did she even pick all that up? Thomas and I said, like, two sentences about it, and we'd kept our voices low.

"How nice," Claudia said. "Since you're heading that way, will you deliver something to Barrett Shaw for us?"

I had intended to avoid Barrett Shaw like a hole in the head, but we *were* going to the Farm, and she would take care of the kids. There was no way to weasel out of it.

"Sure."

Claudia rose, walked over to the small side room, and came back out with a bird cage wrapped with silver wire and covered with a cloth. She lifted the cloth for a second. Inside a small ball of light hovered like a fur pompom made of greenish glow. A will-o'-wisp. Nobody knew for sure what they were, but it took supernatural speed to catch one and a lot of knowledge to contain it. And carrying it around was a really dumb idea, because will-o'-wisps attracted all sorts of weird magical crap to themselves.

"I trust you to get it there safely."

Kate Lennart, the Order's errand girl, at your service. "I'll make every effort to."

I hugged the kids, said my goodbyes, picked up the cage, and Thomas and I escaped the office.

"You don't look happy," he observed.

"It could've gone better," I said. "Will-o'-wisps are expensive, dangerous, and hard to catch. If some merc you didn't know walked into your office, would you trust her to carry it across town and safely deliver it?"

"No. I'd get someone I knew to do it."

"That's what I'm thinking." I strapped the cage into Cuddles' saddle bag.

Had Nick called down to Wilmington and given them a heads-up to expect me? If so, what did this errand mean? Was she trying to put me in my place? Was this a show of trust from Claudia? Was this a message to Barrett intended to communicate that I was allied with the knights? I doubted Barrett would recognize me. I'd never met him.

Maybe I was overthinking this. Maybe Claudia felt that saving

Darin was a good thing, realized that the Farm would hardly welcome us with open arms, and wanted Barrett to understand that she knew why I was showing up on his doorstep.

I climbed into the saddle.

"To the Farm?" Thomas asked.

"To the Farm."

So far I'd run into the Order, and I was about to go and throw a stick into the undead hornet nest that was the People's base in Wilmington. I would need to mind every *P* and *Q* because if they found out who I was, I would never hear the end of it.

ON PAPER, THE FARM LAY LESS THAN 5 MILES AWAY FROM THE chapter, on the other side of the Cape Fear River. Since the Memorial Bridge was no more, the best and fastest way across the river was the ferry, which ran continuously during the daylight. If things went according to plan, we would get there in under an hour. Even in half an hour, if Thomas' horse could keep up with Cuddles, who for unknown and probably abnormal reasons, had the gait of a Tennessee Walker and the speed of one, too.

Things didn't go to plan.

Thomas squinted at the shady-looking captain standing by a small workboat. "What do you mean, the ferry isn't running?"

The captain spat to the side. He wore a grimy gray sweatshirt, equally grimy khaki work pants, and old boots. A beige baseball cap with an embroidered American flag in a shape of a bass covered his hair, and a pair of ancient shades hid his eyes. He hadn't shaved in about a week, and the dark stubble sheathing his narrow chin clearly had beard ambitions.

The workboat behind him looked about as worn and gritty as he did. A flat-bottom aluminum barge, it was about 30 feet long, with a sturdy railing along the flat deck and a narrow rectangular cabin at the stern, just big enough for the captain and maybe a couple of people. Pre-Shift, it would've likely hauled small cargo loads and would easily fit an average-sized truck. Today it was hauling passengers, and the deck had smears of horse manure on it.

We were on the dock, with the stubby remnants of the Memorial Bridge jutting over the river to the left of us. In front of us Cape Fear flowed, its blackwater the color of greenish pewter. A handful of boats braved the crossing, crawling to and from the other bank.

"See the purple?" The captain pointed at the purple flag flying off a mast on the remains of the Memorial bridge. "Dangerous marine life, hazardous conditions. The name's Scully. I'll take you across for $200."

"That's robbery," Thomas ground out. "The ferry is $20."

"Well, the ferry ain't running, and purple flag means hazard pay. I'm takin' a personal risk."

"We can wait for one of those." Thomas nodded at the boats making their way toward us.

"It ain't gonna be cheaper," Scully said. "Besides, I don't see a lot there that can take on two horses."

Cuddles wasn't a horse, but it was beside the point. There was an edge to Thomas' stare. He'd gotten up this morning with a definite plan: either he would get enough money together and buy his son back or he wouldn't. He was afraid to hope for Column A and almost certain he would end up with Column B, and he had put his emotions into a steel-hard grip to cope with it. Instead, he got Column C. We were making unexpected progress toward finding Darin, and he was seeing the first glimmers of light at the end of the tunnel. His control was slipping.

Some part of Thomas still expected that he would have to pay for his son, and he was carrying his life savings on him. He was acutely aware that every dollar he spent was one dollar less for Darin's ransom. Right now, Scully was standing between Thomas and his son, impeding our progress, and he was shaking us down. It was a very dangerous place to be.

The captain was about as trustworthy as an unpiloted vampire. The will-o'-wisp's cage didn't fully fit into the saddlebag, so I had settled for kind of strapping it in, and he'd glanced at it four times since we'd started talking. He was a sailor, and will-o'-wisps loved marshes. Scully would've seen hundreds of them in his time on the water and would know that they went for about $50K apiece. I could see the butt of a crossbow laying on the passenger bench in the boat cabin. He probably had a shotgun or a rifle in there as well.

"Make up your mind," Scully drawled. "You want across or not?"

Any other time I would've waited for a safer option since I had Thomas and two mounts to guard. But we had no time. If the Red Horn had warned Onyx and he warned his buyer, our chances of finding Darin would plummet. There was a fifteen-year-old kid out there held against his will by some asshole, and gods alone knew what was happening to him while we stood on this shore.

Thomas unclenched his jaw.

I tossed a chunk of silver to the captain. Scully snapped it out of the air. Paper money was fragile, but silver was expensive and much more durable. And I'd given him about $50 more than he'd asked.

"Take us across. That's all. Don't get fancy. Keep the bird in hand, and your head attached to your neck."

"Whatever you say." Scully made a small, mocking bow. "Welcome aboard."

I showed Cuddles a carrot, and she clopped her way onto the boat, like it was solid ground. Thomas' horse took a bit more convincing, but in the end everyone boarded, Scully got into his cabin, and we were off.

Enchanted water motors normally made enough noise to raise the dead, but the boat motor was submerged, and the river muffled the sound to a tolerable hum. We weren't moving very fast, but the shore was growing farther away. The green wall of smooth cordgrass sheathed the banks like a fuzzy green blanket. Something large writhed in it. Something thick and brown...

The beast slid toward the water, mashing the cordgrass aside. It resembled a giant leech, three feet thick and six feet long, with a leathery brown hide glistening with water and mud. Its blunt, eyeless head rose, swaying, as if sampling the wind. A round mouth opened, revealing a ring of rectangular nasty teeth leading to a throat studded with barbs. The beast slipped into the water.

A juvenile Tinh Đỉa, a long way off from its original home in Vietnam. Sooner or later, some merc from the local Guild would be coming down here to take care of it. Probably sooner since they grew fast, reached eighteen feet in adulthood, and ate anything that moved. Maybe the city would contract the Order to do it.

I glanced at Scully in his cabin. He'd modified the boat windshield so instead of one glass piece, he had two of them overlapping, and right now he'd slid the left half of it aside. There was only one reason for that modification. It let him shoot without leaving the safety of the cabin. It was a good plan, but a crossbow was wider than the opening, which meant his killing field was pretty narrow.

The boat slid over the dark water. The river teemed with life, and most of the magic it radiated didn't feel friendly.

I moved over to Thomas and murmured, "Go to the right side of the boat and wander toward the cabin."

He didn't give any indication he had heard me.

I walked away from him toward my donkey.

Something bumped the boat in passing.

Cuddles snorted. I patted her muzzle. "I know."

Thomas made his way toward the cabin on the right. Two more steps and he was out of Scully's range.

Thump.

Thump. Thump.

Thump, thump, thump.

"Giant sturgeon going upriver. Nothing to worry about," Scully called out.

The Shift had given a lot of fauna a boost, as if it tried to compensate for the human-wrecked ecosystem. Animals, both common and magic, flourished, and fish were no exception. Atlantic sturgeon now grew to almost 20 feet and topped 1,000 pounds. They were also bottom feeders. Their spawn season was about over, which meant they should be going down river, not up. Something was driving them to the surface and away from the ocean.

The steady hum of the engine gently tapered off.

I stepped closer to the cabin, hanging to the left. I still wanted him to think he had a shot.

The engine died. I dipped my hand into the pouch on my belt and pulled out a handful of the contents in my fist.

Three, two, one…

Scully leveled a crossbow at me. A compact Ten-Point, good brand, designed to bring down medium-sized game. He'd drop a human with one shot.

"Alright, boys and girls, here's what's gonna happen. You bring me the wisp, pass it through this window, and hop on into the water. I'll let your horses out on the shore."

Thomas lunged for the cabin door, grabbed the handle, and yanked. The door remained shut. Scully had locked it.

"Go on!" Scully waved the bow at me from inside the cabin.

"Or what?" I asked.

"Or I'll shoot you or your horse, you dumb bitch."

"She's not a horse. She's a donkey."

"What the hell do I care? Get to it."

"You've thought this through?" I asked.

"Yeah."

I threw a handful of wolfsbane powder into the cabin. Wolfsbane was a shapeshifter deterrent. A shapeshifter caught in it would collapse into sneezing and coughing fits and go scent-blind for a couple of hours. It didn't work as well on humans, but any person suddenly inhaling a cloud of talcum-fine dust would react.

A bright yellow cloud bloomed inside the cabin. Scully choked, staggered back, and sneezed. His head went forward, his crossbow dipped down, and the telltale twang announced a shot fired.

"Aaaaaaa!"

I leaned to look down. Yep. The crossbow bolt pinned his left foot to the deck of the cabin. Captain Scully, Supergenius.

"Fuck! Fuck, fuck, fuck..."

"Unlock the door," I told him.

Thomas smiled.

I glanced at him.

A little light sparkled in Thomas' eyes. "He shot himself in the foot trying to rob us. Literally."

"Yes. Scully, unlock the door. That red puddle by your foot isn't strawberry syrup."

"Fuuuuck!"

"Less cursing, more unlocking, unless you want to keep bleeding."

Scully eyed me like a cornered dog. I unsheathed Sarrat and put it to his throat through the window. "Unlock. The. Door."

He reached over and popped the lock on Thomas' side. Thomas got into the cabin, confiscated the crossbow, tossed it onto the deck, and unlocked my door. I came around and looked at Scully's impaled foot. Judging by what I could see of the shaft, the head had gone clean through his foot and about two inches through the deck. Good crossbow. He was lucky the bolt was wood and not metal.

I sheathed my saber, got my knife out, grabbed the bolt just above the boot, and sliced the shaft with my knife.

Scully yowled.

"Grab him," I told Thomas.

Thomas grabbed Scully by the shoulders.

"You're going to lift your foot off the bolt. I'll help you."

I clasped his boot, and Scully jerked back. "It hurts, you dumb bitch!"

"That's the second time you called me that. I'm going to let it slide, since you're in pain. Don't say it again."

"Why don't we leave him like this until he gets us to the other side?" Thomas suggested.

"I doubt he sterilizes his bolt heads. Who knows what nastiness rode into his foot on that bolt and is now eating him from the inside? We're not complete savages, Thomas."

Scully got a wild look in his eyes and grit his teeth.

"Relax your leg and count to three," I told him.

"One..."

I yanked his foot up. The foot came free. Scully screeched. Thomas muscled him out of the cabin and onto the deck.

"Can you drive the boat?" I asked Thomas.

"Yes. My dad had one."

"You drive, and I'll go watch our sharpshooter friend."

I checked the passenger bench. The storage space under it yielded a first-aid kit that might have been older than me. I took it and walked out onto the deck. Scully had managed to pick himself up and was now leaning against the rail. His foot was bleeding, and a small puddle pooled by him on the deck.

The horse ignored him, while Cuddles gave him her "kicking" eye. If she wasn't tied at the nose of the boat, she would've wandered over toward the cabin and stomped on his injured foot a few times for funsies. I'd seen her take that initiative before a few times.

The boat motor started slowly.

Scully did his best to stare a hole through my face. Sadly, his eyes lacked the lasers he required.

"You ain't shit," he finally spat out.

"You're right, Simo Häyhä." He wouldn't recognize the name. My best friend had named a rifle after him, because he was the deadliest sniper in modern history. "I'm definitely not shit. But you might be. Also, I don't have a hole in my foot. How about you work on that wound before your blood drips into the water?"

I tossed the first-aid kit at him. He caught it and bared his teeth at me. "Fu—"

A green tentacle as thick as my thigh shot out of the river, wrapped around Scully, and yanked him toward the water. Scully dropped the medkit and grabbed onto the railing, clinging to it for dear life.

I lunged forward, Sarrat jumping into my hand almost on its own, and slashed across the tentacle. Blue blood slicked the wound. Barely broke the skin. Damn.

Four more tentacles thrust out of the river, straight up, flinging water into the air. The tentacles slapped onto the deck, one coming straight for me. I dodged left, and it crashed half a foot from me, wrapping all the way across the boat.

I sliced at the tentacle. It was like trying to cut through a car tire. I could saw through it all day and not get anywhere.

Scully howled.

The little vessel groaned, pulled sideways. Cuddles and Thomas' horse screamed in alarm.

I kept slicing.

Thomas' face was a pale mask in the cabin. He was spinning the wheel, but the boat kept moving sideways.

Scully's screech hit a hysterical note.

The boat careened, shuddering, the other side of it rising out of the water.

Screw it. I drew my blade across the back of my arm, wetting it with my blood, sealing the cut the moment after it was made, and stabbed deep into the nearest tentacle. Magic buckled inside me, and I spat the words out. *"Hesaad! Harrsa ut karsaran!" Mine! That which is mine, break!*

The power words tore out of me in a flash of pain and magic. My blood shot through the beast and detonated.

The river exploded. Water shot straight up like a geyser to forty feet high.

The boat landed back onto the surface, rocking.

Chunks of rubbery flesh rained down around us, hitting the deck and the mounts with wet thuds. I lunged toward the front of the boat, grabbed the two sets of reins, and held on.

I had blown my low profile out of the water, and it was now raining down all around me.

Something slimy landed on my head.

We were in the middle of the river. The nearest boat was a good third of a mile away. That should've been enough of a distance to mask the power word usage. Right?

They might not have felt it, but they sure as hell would've seen the result. Curran would be thrilled. Just thrilled. At least I could repair my cuts now. In the old days I would have had to slap a bandage on my arm and then set the damn boat on fire to keep my blood from exposing me.

The chunks still kept falling. The deck was almost completely blue now.

Usually that phrase didn't explode its targets, even with the added punch of my blood. Usually, it just broke bones. This had never happened before. There must not have been any bones for it to break. I would have to discuss it with my aunt during our bi-weekly phone call. She taught me this phrase and didn't mention anything about aquatic creatures bursting. Kind of a crucial detail there.

The boats that were crossing the river reversed course and sped away from us.

If I'd known the monster would explode, I would've used something else. It was supposed to just quietly sink.

Scully gaped at me, still clutching the railing.

"This is your fault," I told him and pulled a long, blue clump off my head.

He cringed.

"Don't move and don't say anything. I mean it. Not a word."

He nodded frantically.

Ten minutes later we disembarked. As soon as we hit the dry land, Scully limped into the cabin, pulled away, made a sharp left turn, and headed up the river as fast as his boat could go.

"You have something in your hair," Thomas said.

I picked another clump out. It felt limp like oyster meat. I tossed it into the river, took my canteen out of Cuddles' saddle bag, and rinsed my hair.

"Better?"

"Some."

I rinsed it a bit more.

"Low profile, huh?" Thomas said.

"Yep. Would you rather I had let that thing pull the boat under?"

He shook his head.

I pictured Curran's face in my head. *Hi, honey, I accidentally exploded some kind of baby kraken in the Cape Fear River in broad daylight in front of a dozen witnesses. Yes, I do remember that I was the one who originally insisted on the lying low thing. Yes, I do recall that you said it would never work. No, it's not funny...*

I put the cap back onto the canteen and slid it into the saddle-bag. "Let's get to the Farm while we still have some daylight left."

[4]

The road was narrow but well maintained. Fields stretched on both sides, fluffy blueberry rows on the left and a wall of corn on the right. The sun was slowly but steadily rolling toward the horizon somewhere behind the corn.

That's what you want, visiting the navigators just before dusk. Ugh.

In my mind's eye, eleven red sparks burned like annoying little embers, five to the right and six to the left. Two vampire teams, each spark an undead piloted by a navigator. We couldn't see them, but they were there, steadily working their way to us.

When my father had created the People, his purposes were complex and layered. He had wanted a network of information-gathering installations and access to a garrison armed with deadly weapons in every major city. Because vampires were expensive to obtain and maintain, he had needed these installations to generate income. He had also required a way to bring talented navigators under his control, train them, and indoctrinate them into a hierarchy with himself at the top of the pyramid. He had strove toward a monopoly on vampire ownership, while also devoting much of his considerable resources to research into undeath and its uses. The truth, which he readily admitted to me, despite his massive ego, was that even though he had originated vampirism, he didn't fully comprehend the mechanism by which it worked.

The People were the answer to all those needs. Their bases performed community outreach, operated entertainment venues, apprehended loose vampires at no charge, and provided an opportunity for the terminally ill to sell their bodies to be infected with the Immortuus pathogen, which would turn them into vampires after death, for a substantial payout to their family. The population at large simply accepted the People, somehow ignoring the fact that they could unleash a horde of lethal monsters in the centers of most cities at any moment.

It was perhaps my father's second greatest confidence scheme. He had managed to convince everyone that the People were perfectly safe, productive contributors to their local community, when a single vampire, piloted by a skilled Master of the Dead, could depopulate ten city blocks in a matter of minutes.

On the left, an undead scuttled into view. Gaunt, hairless, and smeared in purple sunblock, it moved on all fours like its body had never walked upright. It was as if something took a human, bled them dry, skinned them, stripped off all their fat, and then stretched a thick, leathery hide over the bone and muscle. A nightmare come to life. The small cross-body satchel hanging from its left shoulder somehow just made the horror of it worse.

Thomas stiffened a little.

The vamp paid us no mind. It rose to a half crouch, plucked blueberries with stiletto claws, and deposited them into the satchel.

We drew even with it.

The bloodsucker pulled a berry off, and it popped between its claws. A young female voice came from its mouth. "Damn it."

The vamp shook its hand, flinging purple juice off, and plucked another berry.

Plop.

"Damn it."

We rode on. Her voice faded behind us.

"Damn it. Damn it. Damn it..."

"Why use vampires?" Thomas asked quietly.

"Dexterity training. Blueberries are a good measure of control. Squeeze too hard, and they burst. Most good navigators never stop practicing. I know a Master of the Dead who knits elaborate lace socks for practice. Two vamps at a time, perfectly in sync."

Thomas raised his eyebrows.

Another vamp emerged from the berry bushes, looking roughly the same as the one before, except its sunblock was Pepto-Bismol-pink. It set about gathering the berries, but instead of plucking them by claw, this vamp had a pair of tiny manicure scissors, and it snipped the berries one by one.

The team in the corn glided next to us, moving through the stalks just out of our view. Our lovely escort doing their best to stay hidden.

The People's base in Atlanta, headquartered in the Casino, was an all-purpose installation, equal parts research institute, vampire stable, and money machine. Wilmington's Farm was a different beast. It was almost entirely a military installation, conceived by my father as a training facility where promising journeymen were sent to hone their control and learn tactics and team combat. It was the People's boot camp and a convenient reserve of the undead close enough to Atlanta to get there within a day but too far for me to exert any influence over them. They raised livestock and grew feed, and they trained future and current Masters of the Dead.

Unlike a lot of other People offices, the Farm didn't need to interact with the general public to make its money. When the People had fractured into individual groups following my father's exile, the Farm remained exactly as it was. Instead of being subsidized by the Golden Legion, it had simply started charging the individual People offices for its training. My father had given

Barrett Shaw a job, and as far as Barrett was concerned, he would keep doing it until my father told him to stop.

I had to admire the setup. The Farm took up almost all of Eagles Island, about 3,100 acres of it sitting pretty just west of Wilmington, sectioned off from the rest of the state by the Cape Fear River in the east and the Brunswick River to the west. Pre-Shift, there was a three-point road junction in the northeast corner of the island. The junction was still there, although it was now called Vampire Highway. The half-acre buffer zone around Vampire Highway was state land. The rest was the private property of the Farm.

How they put that deal into place, I had no idea. Both the Memorial and the Isabel Holmes Bridges were out, although the Isabel Holmes Bridge was being rebuilt, and stopping ferries from running would be child's play for a man with Barrett's resources. The bridge over Brunswick River was a narrow, arched affair that I could hold by my lonesome against a small army. Parking a team of three undead there meant nobody would cross.

With one command, Barrett Shaw could secure the island and cut Wilmington off from the west side of the state, squeezing the city between his vampires and the Atlantic coast. The lands north of the city had largely devolved into dense wilderness, interrupted by occasional farms. Evacuating would be painful and futile.

The People must've convinced the city leadership or the state that they would defend Wilmington against potential threats. The wolf hid its teeth, so they let it guard their flock.

The fields ended, and a massive facility came into view: a collection of buildings that could've housed a small university complete with a large stadium to the right. No walls. No guards. The Farm didn't need them.

If I closed my eyes, the entire place would glow with red. They had at least 300 vampires. No, more. Another clump of red sparks shimmered deeper south. The Farm was doing quite well for itself.

A small building was at the very front of the campus, facing the road. A big sign marked it as the Visitor Center. Huge square windows, a glass door, and not a single metal bar in sight. Ahh, the privilege of stabling a horde of undead.

"This is far enough," I told Thomas. "Thank you. I'll take it from here."

"If you go in, will you come out?" he asked.

"Yes."

"I'll wait," he said.

"You don't have to. I know you're worried about your family."

"Like you said, your husband will take care of them." Thomas nudged his horse forward. "I will wait."

"Suit yourself."

We dismounted, secured our mounts, I took the will-o'-wisp in the cage out of the saddlebag, and we went inside. The front room could've belonged to an upscale hotel or the reception area of a thriving corporation. The walls were pale marble somewhere on the border of beige and gray, with barely visible darker streaks. A long counter sectioned off the far wall, which was clad in American black granite. Paul had wanted to use a similar stone for our larger living room fireplace, which I vetoed because I hated it. A grouping of sofas and padded chairs occupied most of the floor. The furniture was tasteful, leather, with square angles and wide proportions.

A young woman smiled at us from behind the counter. She wore a blue-green silk blouse with draped sleeves. Her long, dark hair was pulled back into a bun and her makeup was minimal, just a touch of pale lipstick and a hint of eyeliner tracing her hooded eyes.

"How may I help you?"

When outgunned, open with a brick to the face.

"I'm here to discuss a possible breach of the Unnatural Infection Victim Protection Act by a member of this facility. Also,

Claudia Ozburn asked me to drop off this will-o'-wisp for Mr. Shaw, since I was in the neighborhood."

The woman's smile gained a slightly plastic quality. That's right, I'm accusing you of breaching federal law, and the Knight-Protector knows about it. Happy Monday.

"Please take a seat. Would you like some refreshments?"

"No, thank you."

Thomas and I sat. I put the cage with the will-o'-wisp onto the coffee table. The woman disappeared through a door behind the counter.

Thomas was clearly itching to ask some questions, but instead he just sat quietly. Dream client, although I would've preferred that none of this had happened and his son was home instead.

The undead signatures were buzzing about in my head like a swarm of angry hornets. Ugh. The urge to reach out and squish a couple was almost too much.

My first meeting with my father was public and bloody. Despite the somewhat impactful nature of it, very few members of the People outside of my father's inner circle have ever seen me or met me in person. Most of those who witnessed me enter the Swan Palace were dead, killed in dangerous assignments and in the two battles of Atlanta.

All of this was very much by design. My father hadn't wanted me to become a viable alternative to his rule. He had much preferred that I remained a whispered rumor, a long-lost heir who could but probably didn't exist. The moment the Swan Palace visitors had seen me shatter his blood ward, their days became numbered. Only a handful of them had survived, and all of them made it a point to put as much distance between me and themselves as possible and kept their mouths shut.

All that meant was that I could enjoy relative anonymity. I just had to make sure I didn't do anything to announce that I was Roland's daughter.

The vampiric sparks crawled across my mind, stabbing me with their light. Easier said than done.

A man entered through the side door. Average height, average build, dark hair, deep bronze skin, somewhere around thirty. Neat, fit, almost military bearing, clean-shaven. He wore a black jumpsuit loose enough to allow full freedom of movement but tailored enough to double as a military uniform of sorts. The top quarter of his left sleeve, covering the shoulder all the way to mid-biceps, was bright red.

The color had to be an indication of rank. What happened if they went up or down in rank? Did they get a new uniform, or did they rip their sleeve off and replace it?

I squinted. Oh, Velcro. Well, that was a flex. Velcro cost a pretty penny.

"Where is Malone?" the woman asked him softly.

The man shook his head and approached me. Uh-oh. They should've passed me off to HR or the legal department. Personnel in both of those would likely wear suits. The People took their corporate image seriously.

"Director Shaw would like a word," he said.

Straight to the top. Woo.

I picked up the will-o'-wisp, smiled at Thomas, and followed the man out through the front door.

THE FARM REALLY DID RESEMBLE A COLLEGE CAMPUS. IT FELT planned, a complete microcosm, unnaturally clean and carefully managed, with buildings designed by the same team of architects and landscaping arranged with a definite vision in mind. We passed a bookstore and a small café with outdoor seating on the patio, which was mostly empty, except for two groups of patrons. A couple of people wore business clothes. Everyone else had some red on their jumpsuits.

A five-navigator team jogged down the street past us, wearing the same jumpsuits as my escort, each with a narrow yellow stripe on their shoulder. Their vampires loped next to them, keeping a jerky pace.

All five navigators were young, the oldest in their mid-twenties. All five had bloodshot eyes, and the bags under their eyes were big enough to carry my weekly haul from the produce market. The last man, a lanky, glassy-eyed redhead, stumbled. His vampire's eyes flashed bright red. The glow dimmed back to smoldering red-amber, but that flash meant his control was hanging by a hair.

My escort stopped and stepped into the street. The team crashed to a tired stop in front of him. The navigators turned to face him and went to parade rest, their undead sitting on their haunches in front of them.

"Unit ID," he said.

"Yellow Team 2," the leading navigator said. She was short and slight, with long, dark hair put away into a bun, brown eyes, and a wary expression as if she expected a sudden punch to knock her to the ground.

"Name?"

"Journeyman Zhou."

My guide walked down the line and stopped in front of the last man.

"Name?"

"Journeyman Edwards."

"Do you need to tap, Journeyman Edwards?" He said it in a quiet, deliberate way that seemed familiar somehow.

Edwards blanched. "No, sir."

"Infinity," my guide ordered.

The team simultaneously stepped to the side, widening the distance between themselves.

Edwards swallowed. His vampire circled him, weaving between him and the next navigator like a dog dodging poles at an agility competition.

Right, left, right...

Eye flash.

...Left, right...

The vamp's eyes went bright red, the light mad and fueled by bloodlust. Edwards cried out. The undead lunged at the nearest navigator, lightning-fast, and froze, poised on its hind legs, wicked claws spread an inch from the young woman's throat. She shook like a leaf but didn't break formation.

The vamp folded itself back into a crouch with almost mechanical precision, sitting on its haunches. Its mouth opened, and my guide and the vampire spoke in the same voice in stereo.

"Team Leader Zhou, in your opinion, should Journeyman Edwards have tapped?"

Zhou closed her eyes for a long moment and opened them. "Yes, sir."

"Did you order Journeyman Edwards to tap?"

"No, sir."

"Why?"

"Journeyman Edwards has tapped twice already. Tapping a third time would get him kicked from the program, sir."

"So, you prioritized the feelings of your team member over everyone's safety."

It didn't sound like a question.

"Yes, sir," Zhou confirmed.

"Journeyman Zhou, take your team to your superior and inform them that I've relieved you of your post. Journeyman Edwards, report to the personnel office for out-processing."

"Please," Edwards said, his voice a hoarse whisper.

My guide just looked at him.

Edwards turned around, his fists clenched, and marched back the way he came from.

"Dismissed."

The team executed a turn, formed back into a line, and jogged to the right, disappearing between the buildings. Edwards' vampire remained, still sitting on its haunches.

"Harsh," I said.

"But necessary." This time only the guide's mouth moved. He must've decided the undead speaker had served its purpose.

He invited me to keep walking with a small gesture. We resumed walking toward the tall arena looming against the evening sky. Edwards' vampire trailed us, perfectly in sync with our pace, like a loyal, well-trained dog. This man wasn't just a Master of the Dead. He was good enough to head his own office.

"Before a navigator can move to tactics, they must prove their ability to control the undead. We deprive them of sleep, give them contradictory orders, force them to perform nonsensical, menial tasks, all of it designed to simulate the stress of real warfare. They are told they have three chances to tap, which is to admit that they're unable to maintain navigation and ask for a break."

"And if they tap three times?"

"They leave the program, but they can seek readmission in 6 months."

He kept his voice casual and low, nothing suspicious, but unless someone was really close to us, they wouldn't be able to make out the words.

"Tapping is a test in itself," I said.

A navigator who lost control of their vampire in a population center would cause catastrophic casualties. Even if they notified the People immediately, acquiring control required close physical proximity. There would still be a slaughter.

My guide nodded. "One must experience being on the verge of losing control at least once and demonstrate sound judgement even when faced with serious consequences. Journeyman Edwards will not be returning to the Farm."

The arena was directly in front of us, silhouetted against the glowing sky like a foreboding citadel.

"After all, not everyone is fit to pilot *utukku-dami*."

Blood demon. Words from an ancient language. When infused with magic, they became words of power, but when spoken like this, casually, they resurrected echoes of the Kingdom of Shinar.

Alarm shot through me. I kept walking, keeping my breathing even, and glanced at him again. Calm, brown eyes, smart, observant. I identified the similarities now, the vaguely familiar proportions of his face, the line of his eyebrows, the cheekbones, the brown skin with an almost golden undertone, and the voice. Especially the voice.

"Sharrim...You are young," a deeper voice murmured from my memories with the same steady cadence. *"You have the power but lack control. Think of all the things he could teach you. Think of the secrets that would open to you."*

My father was born in our pre-history. Before our Shift, there had been another, the one that had ended the previous magic age and ushered in our technological era. The tech-Shift drove my father into hibernation, and he wasn't the only one who'd gone to sleep. He'd chosen a very short list of people he trusted to support him in the new age. One of them was a quiet man who appeared to be in his sixties. He came from an old family. His father had served my father, as had his father, and his father, and on and on. His real name was Jushur, but my father called him Akku. The Owl.

Quiet, unassuming, always pretending to be less than he was, Jushur went by many different names. He'd moved through the People's ranks, never drawing attention to himself, excelling at being overlooked and dismissed. He was my father's secret eyes and ears. He'd served the most troublesome of Legati of the Golden Legion and had kept an eye on Hugh d'Ambray during his tenure as Warlord. When trouble brewed somewhere, Jushur would already be there, on the sidelines, anticipating the crisis and taking subtle steps to deal with it. He had six children, some born in the old age and others in ours, and all of them were just like him, fanatically loyal to my father and his bloodline.

I had discounted him even though he'd spoken to me directly three times. After my father had decided he did want to speak to me again—it took him almost three years—he finally told me about Jushur one night over beer and doughnuts, while he was rearranging the constellations in the sky of his realm to be more aesthetically pleasing.

The man walking next to me looked like a younger version of Jushur and sounded just like him. And he wanted me to know who he was.

Well, wasn't that just peachy.

Ahead the gates of the arena stood wide open. As we came closer, a sheepish-looking navigator team with green stripes on their jumpsuits led a brown cow out of it. A big, white paw print marked the cow's butt. Weird way to tag the People's cows, but okay.

We walked through the gates. The floors of ancient arenas were made of wood and covered with a layer of sand to absorb the blood. This arena was stone, no padding. Every drop of blood was a precious resource.

Two men waited on the arena floor, near the gates. Behind them three vampires crouched in a row, still like statues.

The first man, on my right, was young, in his twenties, tall and thin. Everything about him seemed slightly too long: his dark hair, his nose, his chin. A single red stripe marked the shoulder of his jumpsuit. I'd cracked the code by this point. Red meant cadre, permanent staff of the Farm, and the more red you had, the higher your rank. This guy was pretty low in the chain of command.

A man like Barrett Shaw would have either known or suspected that one of his journeymen was up to no good. There was no reason for this guy to be in the arena if he was just some random navigator.

Hello, Onyx. We finally meet. I've come to chat about a child you sold like livestock.

The other man had two red shoulders on his jumpsuit. He was

also tall, but unlike Onyx, who was thin to the point of looking fragile, this man was muscled like a decathlon athlete, lean and hard. An all-purpose build, equally fast, strong, and flexible, and the way he stood told me he had good balance. Onyx I could fold in half like paper. That man would dodge a fast punch and come back swinging.

He was probably close to forty, but it was hard to tell. His hair, a deep brown, umber shade, was cut just long enough to style, although he hadn't bothered. No gray yet. He had probably started his day clean-shaven this morning, but now a five o'clock shadow darkened his square jaw. A tall forehead, prominent nose, full mouth, and dark green eyes under thick eyebrows. Not a conventionally handsome face, but a powerful one. The kind of face that would make you rethink your strategy.

The green eyes took my measure. He had an unsettling, direct gaze, as if he were looking at something specific inside you. Barrett Shaw. In the flesh.

I stared back, trying to look blank. *Look all you want. There is nothing to see here.*

Jushur's son stood to the side at parade rest, his undead sitting by him.

Barrett smiled. It was a pleasant, affable smile. Perfectly cordial. "Welcome to the Farm."

"Thank you."

One of the vampires sprinted at full speed toward me, its eyes red.

Cute.

The undead slid to a stop a couple of inches from my feet. I held out the will-o'-wisp cage and nodded at Barrett.

"Your parcel. Claudia Ozburn says hello."

"She always sends the nicest things."

The undead took the cage from me and carried it off.

Barrett Shaw was still smiling.

I should've flinched when the undead ran at me. Most people

would've flinched. I was positioning myself as either a merc or a knight of the Order. Vampire removal wasn't something mercs did often, and a knight would've called him on his bullshit or taken a defensive stance. Either way, I should've reacted.

Even if I had tried to fake a reaction, it would've been obvious. My acting skills were severely lacking.

Barrett wasn't speaking. Ryan Kelly, a Master of the Dead from Atlanta, once referred to him as Gator Mouth, and now I knew why. That warm smile was a tornado siren, announcing a whirlwind of destruction coming my way. This had become about me, and I needed to deflect his attention and get access to Onyx, because he was our only link to Darin. I had to explain why I hadn't freaked out.

"How do you like it? The Farm? Did Rimush give you a tour on the way here?"

An idea popped into my brain. It was a terrible idea, but it was the only one I could think of. "It's very organized. Even the cohorts are color-coded."

Despite the name, the Golden Legion didn't have cohorts, and neither did the People. There was only one military force accustomed to dealing with vampires that used the term *cohorts*.

Take the bait, take the bait, take the bait…

Barrett's affable expression stayed pleasant. "You're a long way from Kentucky."

I blinked a couple of times to indicate surprise. Kate the Thespian. Hand me my Oscar. "Well, that didn't take long. The Preceptor and I parted ways."

"And why is that?"

"I've got a problem with authority."

Hugh's Iron Dogs used to be my father's counterpoint to the Golden Legion. His left and right arms, trained to kill each other if necessary. Hugh was now an independent operator, and if Barrett checked with him—which was highly unlikely—he would cover for me. As soon as I got home, I would have to call

Hugh and let him know. He'd get a good laugh out of this, the jackass.

The intensity of Barrett's smile eased a little. I had given him a believable story. A former Iron Dog would be a highly trained, skilled, disciplined killing machine. If Claudia became aware of one operating independently, it would make sense that she would try to recruit her. It would also make sense that after walking away from Hugh D'Ambray, said Iron Dog wouldn't be eager to take orders again, so Claudia would take it easy, by talking her into running an errand or two. Mystery solved.

"Ms. Ozburn is marking her territory," Barrett said, as if to himself. "Very well. What brings you here?"

"I'm looking for a kidnapped child. Onyx brokered the sale."

Barrett nodded and looked at the journeyman. "Did you hear that?"

Onyx gave me a defiant stare. "I didn't do it."

"Jace gave you up," I said.

"He's lying."

I turned to Barrett and spread my arms.

Barrett rubbed the bridge of his nose. "And this is where you've fucked up. You should've asked who Jace was. Because there is no reason for you to associate with a mid-level Red Horn boss. But you didn't. Because we both know you've been doing some shady shit. Malone warned you about it, didn't he?"

Onyx opened his mouth.

"Don't," Barrett said. All the pleasantness evaporated from his face in an instant.

Onyx swallowed.

"You brought your shady shit here. To *my* island. Now there is a mercenary asking questions and the Order is aware of it. You have a fucking problem. How are you going to fix it?"

Panic sparked in Onyx's eyes. The older of the two remaining vampires charged me.

The world slowed to an underwater crawl. The vampire was

coming for me, mouth gaping, fangs ready to bite and tear, driven by Onyx's rattled mind.

If I killed it, the backlash would fry Onyx, tuning him into a vegetable. He wasn't taking any precautions, and a sudden ending of the connection between the navigator and the undead destroyed the navigator's ego.

If I took control of the vampire, I might as well have just cut my vein and started making blood armor right there. Not only would I not save Darin, but I could kiss any hope of a calm life in Wilmington goodbye.

The vamp was almost on me.

I had one chance at this. No do-overs.

I pulled Sarrat from its sheath, grasped the undead's mind with my magic, ripped it away from Onyx, and let it go, all in the same fraction of a second. The journeyman had no time to react. The vamp's eyes flared bright red. It was already running, and I was directly in front of it, a convenient target with a heartbeat. It leaped, claws spread for the kill.

I sliced across its forelimbs, spun out of the way, and slashed at its neck, cleaving the head from the body in a single blow.

The beheaded body ran a few more steps and crumpled onto the stone. The head rolled across the arena's floor.

Onyx stared at the dead vampire, trying to process what had happened. He wasn't sure who took the vampire away from him. Both Rimush and Barrett were Masters of the Dead. It could've been either of them, and now he didn't know how to react.

I breathed in, slow and deep. If Barrett caught me, there would be hell to pay.

Barrett wasn't looking at me. He was staring at his journeyman, and his eyes shivered with rage. It had worked. He'd thought Onyx had bailed, abandoning the undead in the middle of the attack, because he got scared that I'd kill it.

"I don't mind cleaning house," I said into the silence. "But I have to charge."

Onyx opened his mouth.

I flicked the blood off my blade. "Who did you sell Darin to?"

He took a step back.

I started toward him. Barrett said nothing. Good for me.

"You've broken the First Covenant. The People will not protect you. Tell me where the boy is, and I will spare your life."

"I didn't," Onyx stammered. "I didn't make him into a vampire. He's alive."

"The First Covenant doesn't just cover making people undead against their will. The First Covenant forbids slavery in all its forms. 'There must be free will.' That is the first and most sacred pledge."

The Shinar had been mostly a free kingdom, but it was also a cosmopolitan place where many travelers did business. My great grandfather had outlawed slavery among Shinar citizens, and yet there had been thousands of slaves in the kingdom, brought there by foreign dignitaries and traders. When my father woke up post-Shift, codifying freedom of choice was his first decision and the first law he passed onto the People.

Roland had wanted to impose his will on everyone, but he had also wanted everyone to obey him because they loved him and agreed with him.

I reached striking distance. Onyx stayed where he was, glancing at me, then at Barrett, then at me again.

"You put in a custom order for a child to be stolen off the street and you sold him. That is slavery. You're a human trafficker. Scum."

I raised Sarrat and aimed it at his throat. The blade smoked, feeding on the vampire blood still coating the saber. Thin tendrils of white vapor slid off the pale metal.

"I'm not a patient woman. Who bought the boy?"

Onyx sucked in a lungful of air. "It doesn't matter anyway. He'll kill you. His name is Aaron."

"Last name?"

"Just Aaron. He's a god."

Oh goodie. "Where can I find this god named Aaron?"

"Emerald Wave."

"And what is that?"

Onyx licked his lips nervously. "A cruise ship. It sank off the north end of Figure Eight Island. That's his base."

"Why did he want Darin? Why that particular kid?"

"He buys anyone who can stay under water longer than normal. That's all I know."

"How long has Aaron been buying kids like Darin?"

"For three years."

Gods appeared during flares, extremely potent magic waves that came every 7 years, but they also showed up during random magical events. Three years ago there was a Night of the Shining Seas that coincided with or triggered a particular strong magic wave. And it had an especially strong effect on marine creatures. People called it the Night of the Shining Seas, because the oceans had glowed so bright, it looked like an inverted sunrise.

I slid Sarrat back into its sheath and took three steps back.

Onyx looked at Barrett. "I can explain."

Barrett smiled and raised his eyebrows.

"I owe money to Lunar Crown," Onyx stammered.

Wilmington's largest casino. People did screwed-up shit for three reasons: love, revenge, or greed. Greed far outnumbered the other two.

"I just needed to pay off the debt, that's all..."

Barrett gave him an encouraging nod.

"I never did anything..."

The remaining undead still sitting on the sidelines moved so fast, he might as well have teleported. A dark blur shot past Onyx. The journeyman stopped in mid-word. His mouth hung open in a slack *O*.

His stomach split in half and his intestines fell onto the stone by his feet.

The journeyman gagged. Blood gushed from his mouth. He choked on it, coughed, sending a cloud of bloody spray out, and collapsed.

Barrett's eyes turned distant the way they did when a Master of Dead spoke through a faraway undead. "Blue Team 7, your feed is in the arena."

He had piloted another vampire through this entire conversation. Masters of the Dead who could control two undead at the same time were rare. Just that ability alone had guaranteed a ticket to the Golden Legion when my father was in power.

Onyx made a gurgling noise.

"What's your name?" Barrett asked me.

"Kate."

"A word of advice, Kate. Don't come to my island again."

For a second, I thought of doing things the way my aunt would've done them. And then I remembered why we had moved to Wilmington.

"I'll do my best," I told him, turned, and walked toward the gates.

Rimush fell in step with me. As we exited the arena, 5 undead galloped through the gates, streaming past us to the bloody body on the floor.

[5]

The sunset slowly burned in the west, cooling to dark red and purple. Dusk had claimed the fields of Eagles Island. Thomas and I rode down the same road that had brought us here. A lone vampire was trailing us through the corn, keeping a lot of distance.

"I know where the Emerald Wave is," Thomas said. "Never heard of Aaron though."

And that was strange. If Aaron was a deity, a prophet, or an avatar, he would proselytize. That's how their kind powered up. How was it that Thomas who, by his own admission, was born and raised in Wilmington, had never heard of him or the cult?

"When was the last time you saw the Emerald Wave?"

He thought about it. "Years. The ocean in that area is strange and dangerous."

"When did that start?"

"About three or four years ago."

"Since the Night of the Shining Seas?"

He nodded. "Yes, now that I think about it."

Hm. "Have you heard of anything specific? Any incidents involving people around the Emerald Wave?"

"There are always stories. Supposedly, that ship has a hole in it that can only be seen from inside of it and it's full of monsters."

Peachy.

Thomas checked my face, trying to see what I was thinking.

"The important thing is that Darin is probably alive," I said. "Water breathing is relatively rare. This Aaron needs him for something."

Unless he was sacrificing water breathers to some weird deity, but that wasn't a possibility I would raise with Thomas now.

"Do you think he's really a god?"

"No. Gods can't usually manifest outside of flares. Typical magic waves don't pack enough juice. Also, if the magic falls while a god is in our world in the flesh, they would suffer a lot of damage. They can't exist in physical form during tech. It would take them decades, possibly generations, to build enough power through faith to manifest again."

"But they could? If the wave was strong enough?"

"Theoretically. They won't though. Gods are cowards."

The blueberry bushes ended. Marsh hugged the roadway, clumps of the smooth cordgrass blending together into a wall of green.

Watching Onyx slide around in his own blood on the floor of the arena bothered me. He was a child trafficker. The grimy cages at Red Horn said that he deserved everything he got.

It still bothered me.

He wasn't mine to punish. My aunt would have congratulated me on finally learning some discipline. My father would have turned it into a deep examination of his own altruistic impulses and how they eventually led to his downfall and then lectured me to not repeat his mistakes.

I had to let it go. Obsessing about it would only pull me back onto a very dangerous road. It led to claiming territory, and building towers, and people who pledged their lives to me in exchange for a promise of power and immortality. That wasn't the future I wanted. For myself or for my family.

Something rustled ahead in the marsh. I halted Cuddles. Thomas followed my lead.

The cordgrass parted, and three men emerged onto the road. They moved with the familiar, easy grace of shapeshifters. One of them carried a bucket. And the shortest of them carried a claymore on his back.

Gods damn it all to hell and back. *Don't see us. Don't.*

The three shapeshifters caught our scent and turned to look at us in unison. Three pairs of eyes caught the light of the dying sunrise and shone, one green and two yellow.

The green-eyed claymore user stood up straight. He was short but muscled like a wrestler. "Consort?"

Of all people in the whole wide world to run into.

"Consort!" The shapeshifter dropped to one knee and smacked his fist into his chest. "It's you!"

Why me?

The shapeshifter on his right dropped to one knee as well. The other guy, the one with the bucket, stared at me, wide-eyed.

"Get up, Keelan," I hissed.

The claymore guy jumped to his feet from kneeling position and trotted over, his eyes shining.

"We've been over this. I'm not the Consort. Dali is the Consort now."

Keelan smiled at me with slightly deranged devotion, his blond hair, wet with Cape Fear's dark water, sticking to his face and neck. "You will always be the Consort to me."

My left eye twitched. I slapped my hand over it.

His real name was Caolan Comerford, but he'd changed it when he came to the States. Other Irish people pronounced it as *Kaylin* or *Kwaylan,* Americans called him *Cowlan,* and correcting people got in his way, so he settled on *Keelan* because it sounded cool and was something he could live with.

Keelan claimed to have descended from the werewolves of Ossory, a mythical Irish shapeshifter kingdom that was said to flourish in Ireland pre-Norman invasion. For a while, I wasn't sure he was even Irish, since he played up the charming Celtic-rogue thing so much. But according to Curran, there might have been something to his Ossory claims, because Keelan was abnormally gifted as a werewolf. He had a huge warrior form, could keep it up for a long period of time, could talk while in it, and was absolutely lethal in a fight.

I'd interacted with thousands of shapeshifters in my life, and Keelan was the only shapeshifter who fought with a claymore. In the warrior form. The first time I met him, we were in the middle of a skirmish, and he just kind of waded into it. His claymore was 55 inches long, and he himself was 66 inches tall. He had pulled it off his back, looked around, and suddenly this enormous werewolf spilled out and started swinging the claymore, one-handed. It was all offense. He had zero sword training until me. He had just whipped the claymore around like it was a club, and it hadn't hindered him any, because when a giant werewolf waved around 6 pounds of sharpened metal, it cleared his killing field in record time. It took me almost two years to make him into a half-decent swordsman.

"What are you doing here, Consort?" Keelan asked, petting Cuddles.

"I should be asking you that question. Why are you sneaking into the Farm? Are you trying to start a war?"

The shapeshifter with the bucket hid it behind him.

"What's in the bucket?" I asked.

"Umm," Keelan said.

Keelan had come to us a few months after our trip to the Mediterranean. He had been looking for something to do with his life, and once he'd heard the story of the Beast Lord and his glorious quest to obtain panacea for his pack, he decided to check us out. The moment he had seen Curran in a warrior form, Keelan decided he had found his purpose for living. Somehow my husband was the answer to everything Keelan was searching for. Curran, recognizing talent, had admitted him to the Pack on the condition he would give us 10 years.

And then Curran and I walked away from the Pack. Curran was Keelan's favorite person, and I was his second favorite person, because I taught him how to use his claymore and because I was Curran's mate. Keelan tried to separate with us, but Jim wouldn't let him go until his contract was up. He counted on Keelan to counterbalance Desandra, the alpha of Clan Wolf. Except Keelan wanted nothing to do with being an alpha of the wolves. One time Desandra lost her patience and straight out asked him if he would ever make a bid for her spot, and he told her that only an idiot would want that job, because life was far too short for that kind of bullshit. Both Jim and Desandra tried to pull him to their respective sides, but Keelan proceeded to half-ass every task they had given him and was insufferably apathetic about werewolfing in general and following their orders in particular.

Although headquartered in Atlanta, the Pack claimed a good chunk of the southern Atlantic seaboard as their territory. Wilmington, close to that territory's northern border, was one of the most dangerous areas because of Barrett and the Farm. The Pack maintained a minimal presence here, less than 20 people total, but all of them were highly skilled combat shapeshifters. Almost every promising render did a tour here if they wanted to move up, so when the alpha in charge of the Wilmington sub-pack had gotten herself killed, Desandra nominated Keelan as her replacement to get him out of her hair, and Jim, who'd given up on Keelan by that point, shipped him off.

And now he was sneaking onto the Farm with a bucket.

"What's in the bucket?" I repeated.

Keelan fluttered his eyelashes at me. "The thing is…"

The cow. The cow coming out of the arena with a big-ass paw print on its butt. "Is that paint?"

Keelan surrendered to his fate. "Yes."

"Please tell me that you aren't tagging Barrett's cows with your paws. Tell me you are not doing it."

"I'm not doing it." Keelan nodded. "He is."

The guy with the bucket gave me a small, hesitant wave.

"It's tradition," Keelan said. "When new people come here from Atlanta, they tag the cows. Just to remind them we're watching. It keeps the navigators on their toes."

"I just saw a tagged cow," I growled. "Why are you still here?"

"That was Selina yesterday. Today it's Hakeem's turn. We got two new people this time." Keelan held up two fingers in case I couldn't count.

My face must've been terrible, because Keelan raised his hands up. "It's perfectly safe. I'm going to grab a cow and run with it to the left and Andre is going to grab another cow and run right. While they are chasing us, Hakeem will tag what's left. They're not expecting us for a second night in a row."

At times like this I wished I was still the Consort because I could just order them to leave, and they would. A bloodbath would be avoided.

"Tonight is not the night. I just pissed Barrett off, and there is an undead trailing us."

Keelan's eyes flashed green. "Do you need us to...?"

"I have no right to tell you what I need. I'm not part of the Pack. But I would appreciate an escort off the Farm."

"Oh, we would be delighted." Keelan's voice came out as a guttural snarl. "Protect the Consort."

The shapeshifters formed up around us, with Keelan by my side and the two others bringing up the rear in a triangular formation. We started down the road.

"So what brings you to the Farm, Consort?" Keelan asked.

How could I put this to keep consequences to a minimum...

"She's helping me find my son," Thomas said.

"So sorry he's missing," Keelan said. "How do you two know each other?"

Mayday, mayday...

"We—" I started, trying to make something up.

"My brother is remodeling their home," Thomas said. "They bought Fort Kure."

Damn it.

Keelan's eyes blazed. "Does that mean the Beast Lord is here?"

There was no point in lying. "Yes."

"Here in Wilmington?"

"Yes."

Keelan nodded. "And this house this man's brother is remodeling, will it be a permanent residence?"

"Yes."

Keelan hopped in place and darted into the corn. We kept riding.

Thomas looked at me.

"He needs a moment," I told him. "Please let me answer the questions next time."

"You didn't tell me you were the Consort."

"I'm not the Consort," I growled. "I haven't been the Consort for 9 years."

"I didn't think you were a shapeshifter, but now I see it," Thomas said. "You sound like one."

Behind me Andre made a strangled noise that sounded a lot like an aborted snicker.

Keelan jumped out from the corn and trotted over to his spot by Cuddles. "Why is the Beast Lord not with you?"

"Go ahead, tell him," I told Thomas.

"The Red Horn gang is going to attack Fort Kure tonight," Mr. Loose Lips said.

Keelan smiled. The moon slipped out from behind the clouds and filled his eyes with its light.

"Thomas' family is hiding at Fort Kure," I said. "If you help us across the river and take Thomas back to the fort, you might get there in time for some action."

Keelan smiled, showing me all of his teeth. "It will be an honor."

Yep, I totally passed the buck to Curran. Nope, I didn't feel any guilt about it.

"I thought we agreed I would come with you," Thomas said.

"Things changed. Onyx was a trafficker, but he was also Barrett's journeyman. He was good enough to be part of the Farm's cadre, his permanent staff. Onyx understood power because he witnessed it daily. When he told me about Aaron, there was reverence in his voice. That man may or may not be a god, but he must be packing some serious magic power. If you come with me, I will have two targets to protect, you and Darin. You're going to have to trust me."

Thomas' mouth turned into a hard, flat line.

"I've seen her kill a dragon," Keelan told him in a confidential tone.

Thomas jerked, startled.

"Oh, it was glorious." The werewolf raised his hand, drawing a wide arc across the sky. "The world was smoke and fire. The dragon spat flames like a jet of napalm to and fro. People died where they stood, and their bodies turned to ash. And she ran up its head and thrust two swords into the dragon's eyes while her husband tore out its throat."

Thank you, Keelan, for stabbing my last hope for anonymity through the heart. "You should talk less."

Keelan winked at Thomas. "If anyone can get your boy, she is it. And he'll be overjoyed that his dad is in one piece. Trust in the Consort. I do and I haven't regretted it yet."

Getting across Cape Fear proved to be surprisingly easy because the ferry was now running. According to the captain, a juvenile Sargasso Sea kraken had come into the river, probably due to inexperience, and some fool had blown it clear out of the water, causing a feeding frenzy. Nobody knew how. Crazy what people got up to nowadays.

Thomas had given me detailed directions. I was to take Market Street heading northeast to Porter's Neck, then make a right at the old Walgreens that now was half-pharmacy, half-apothecary, onto Porter's Neck Road. Then I'd make another right onto Edgewater Club, then a left onto Bridge Road, and another left onto Siren Call once I got to Figure Eight Island. About 22 miles. Give or take 3 hours, with some delays built in. The sun had finally set, so it was around 8:30 pm or so. I should get there by midnight.

We parted ways. Keelan, Thomas, and the other two shapeshifters headed south. They would swing by their secondary HQ in Veteran's Forest and pick up more "friends," as Keelan put it, before heading to our place. I wished Keelan good luck, he somberly told me to "stay safe," and I went east on Market Street.

According to the archival records, pre-Shift Market Street was a busy place, a typical small-southern-city kind of road. Hotels, auto parts stores, restaurants, little plaza strips, most buildings one story, maybe two, flanked by generous parking lots. Some of that was still there, but the landscape had changed. Buildings occurred in clumps, with wide killing zones around them in case something weird crawled out of the encroaching woods and decided to sample some two-legged cuisine. A lot of parking lots had fences.

I reached a Food Lion with a large parking lot defended by a guard in a tower. The place was probably about to close—most stores didn't stay open after dark. There was a small restaurant adjacent to it, lit up by blue feylanterns. The sign on it said, "7 to 11." A smaller sign offered breakfast all day. Perfect.

I rode into the parking lot, tied Cuddles to the rail put in front of the restaurant for that purpose, and walked in. The restaurant was tiny, only five tables, all empty. A fast-food style counter cut the kitchen off from the dining area. Above it hung pictures of the dishes with prices: eggs, bacon, sausage, hash browns…

A middle-aged woman, with black, curly hair put away into a round bun and cool tint to her brown skin, came to the counter and gave me a friendly smile.

"What will it be?"

I put $50 worth of silver onto the counter. "Can I use your phone?"

She picked up the silver, reached below the counter, and set the phone onto it. "Got a long night ahead of you?"

How did she know? "Probably."

She nodded and disappeared into the kitchen.

I tried the phone. Dial tone. Score.

I dialed Hugh's number. The phone rang. And rang. And rang…

There was a click and Hugh's voice said, "Yes?"

"It's me."

"Everything okay?"

"Yeah. Did you know the bone-breaking command can explode krakens?"

"Yes."

What the hell. "And you didn't tell me?"

"Did you blow up a kraken?"

"Maybe."

He laughed into the phone. "Is Wilmington still standing?"

"Last I checked."

The woman returned, put a cup of coffee with creamer in front of me and a plate with a small apple Danish, smiled again, and went away.

I took a whiff of apple, cinnamon, and coffee and almost cried with happiness. I'd have to remember this place.

"I went to see Barrett."

"Why?"

"Something came up."

"Does he know who you are?"

"No." I bit into my Danish, poured too much cream into my coffee, and took a big gulp. "I might have pretended to be one of your people."

"Run that by me again?"

"I let Barrett think I was a former Iron Dog."

He guffawed.

"Laugh it up, why don't you?"

"Why?" Hugh managed finally.

"He ran a vampire at me at full speed and I forgot to flinch."

"Aha. And why did you leave my stellar leadership?"

"Apparently I have a problem with authority."

"That checks out. I'll add you to the roll. Lennart or Daniels? Or make something up?"

"Make something up, please."

I took another bite.

The humor drained from Hugh's voice. "Barrett is only dangerous when he smiles and when he doesn't."

"Ha-ha."

"I mean it. Stay clear if you can."

"How good is he?" I took another bite.

"Better than a few Legati I knew."

During my father's rule, the Golden Legion consisted of the best Masters of the Dead, the most talented and deadly, and the Legatus that led it was the strongest of all of them. My father promoted rigorous competition and prioritized strength and talent. The position of Legatus had large turnover, and nobody had yet to retire from it.

"Your buddy Ghastek," Hugh said. "Powerful but too smart for his own good. He thinks too much, and it makes him predictable. Barrett's a thinker too, but nobody knows what makes him tick. He doesn't form alliances. He doesn't respond to threats. It's very difficult to provoke him on purpose, but sometimes he reacts with overwhelming violence to minor shit. If he found out who you are, it might be 'you killed my master, prepare to die' or 'the King is out, long rule the Queen.' I have no idea which he'll pick, and I wouldn't bet a dime either way."

I sighed and drank more of my coffee.

"What does *he* say about it?" Hugh asked.

"Nothing. I haven't asked him. I try to not involve him in my business."

"That's for the best."

"Does your wife know of any water gods active around Wilmington?"

"Why is it that any time a freaky deity pops up somewhere, all of you call my wife?"

"Do you really want me to answer that question?"

"...Good point. Hold on, I'll ask."

I held the phone away from my ear.

"HEY, HONEY? DO YOU KNOW ABOUT ANY WATER GODS IN WILMINGTON?"

How Elara put up with him I would never know. Then again, I married a man who occasionally turned into a lion in his sleep, so I had no room to judge. I finished my Danish.

"She says she doesn't know of anything recent. With Wilmington being an international port, it's hard to say."

"Please tell her thank you."

"A lot of Irish in Wilmington," Hugh said.

"Yeah. I've been thinking about that."

"It could be a god or it could be something else, and either way, it's likely dangerous. Watch yourself."

"Thanks for the pep talk."

"Whatever you do, don't feed it to Curran."

"Ha-ha."

"Call me if you need help. Gods know you could use it."

"If I did call you, what would you do? You've gone soft in your country lord life, in your keep, with your wife baking delicious desserts for you and your gang of children."

"That's good. I'll remind you of that next time you call. And by the way, you can call even when you don't need something. And you can visit."

"I know. Take care."

"You too."

We did visit, eight months ago. Which was why Paul had had to work extra hard to convince Curran that there was absolutely no way to put a moat around our new residence. He still wanted it and swore he'd find a way somehow.

I finished the last swallow of my delicious coffee and went on my way.

As soon as we left the Food Lion parking lot, Cuddles picked up the pace, clopping her way on the crumbling highway like she had some place to be and needed to get there. Horses could be convinced to go faster or slower, but donkeys had a mind of their own, so I gave thanks to the donkey gods and enjoyed the ride.

Eventually we left the city behind and entered the wooded stretch that separated Wilmington proper from the little town of Porter's Neck. Before the Shift, they were part of the same metro, but the hazards brought by the magic waves made the towns contract to their own boundaries. Here woods hugged the road, birches, maples, magnolias, all magic-fed to record size. Keeping the forest at bay was a constant fight, and the humans didn't always win it.

The moon lit my way, its light pouring from the sky. The road ahead almost glowed. Things tracked my progress from the gloom between the trees, their eyes shining in every color. Sometimes instead of a pair, it was one giant eye, sometimes three, set in a triangle. One time it was eight, high in the tree, glowing with eerie magenta. If a giant spider decided to jump onto my head, I'd have a devil of a time convincing Cuddles to keep going in the right direction.

The eyes blinked out on both sides of the road, as if snuffed out by a gust of wind. Hurried rustling announced several furry creatures beating a very fast retreat. I glanced behind me. A vampire crouched on the road. This one was old, gristled and leathery, with claws the size of curved paring knives. Its ruby eyes stared at me with unblinking focus.

About time. It had followed me all the way from the Farm, its presence an annoying red spark on the edge of my mind.

The undead stood up straight. Cartilage crunched as the joints realigned themselves to a posture that was no longer natural. The vampire walked over and took a knee.

"Sharratum," the undead intoned in Rimush's voice.

Sighing wouldn't have been politic. "Just Kate, son of Akku. I renounced that title. And all that went with it."

"It's who you are. You cannot renounce it any more than you can renounce being human."

This would be a complicated conversation. "Join me."

The undead shifted back to all fours, and we started down the road side by side.

"What do you want?" I asked.

"To serve you."

"But I don't want to be served."

Rimush's voice was slightly mournful. "Some rulers wear the crown with pride because they see it as a prize they have won. Some take it as their due, never doubting that it should be theirs. Yet others chafe under it, for it is heavy and the weight of many souls clings to its gold. It is those who push away the power who end up benefitting their people the most."

"I'm not fit to rule."

The vampire sighed. "And yet, rule you must."

"Why?"

"Because your people need you."

"How are you my people?" My people were back at Fort Kure.

"Your father brought us into this unfamiliar, new world.

Everything we know is gone. Our kingdom is a distant memory. Our temples and monuments are gone. The resting places of our ancestors have vanished, and their names are lost to time. Even the land is not the same. He promised us he would rebuild our nation, that he would be our shelter and our guide, and now he is gone."

And he was gone because I made it happen.

"We didn't ask for this. We didn't choose to awaken. We were called to serve and dedicate ourselves to something greater, yet we're left with ashes. We are alone, abandoned and adrift in this new foreign age. You are born of it. Who will protect us and lead us? Who else will guide your people and give us a purpose so we do not become lost?"

Every sentence was an arrow loaded with guilt.

If I could have gotten my hands on my father right this second, I would have shaken him until his teeth rattled in his head, while pointing at the vampire and yelling, "Look what you did!"

"You would be better off paying your respects to my aunt."

"Errahim has her own people. We're not welcome there."

True. Even before my father and aunt had gone to sleep, they maintained separate administrations and staff. Namtur and co. wouldn't react well to Akku and his family butting in.

"Besides, your aunt has chosen to bow her head to a different power. It's not a power we wish to serve."

They knew. How in the world had they found out? Erra's involvement with the federal government was so well hidden, those closest to her didn't even think about it.

"I'm sorry that my father brought you here and left you to fend for yourselves. He is a flawed man, who felt crushing guilt over the demise of his kingdom and became blinded with power and desperation. You're right. He is gone now. This is a new world. The time of our fathers has passed. You don't need to serve me, Rimush. You don't need to serve anyone. The Shinar is over."

Rimush smiled with the vampire's mouth. "The Shinar we knew was over when your father took the throne."

"Then why are you here? Why are you trying to follow our faulty bloodline? Don't you want to be free?"

The vampire looked up at the sky. "It is because I'm free that I'm here."

"I don't understand."

"Shinar began in a time of great darkness, in a land torn by war and besieged by monsters. It was a beacon of hope and light, where the weak were protected and the strong found the purpose of their lives. I grew up with legends of that time, of heroes who selflessly fought, sacrificed, and struggled to find a better way to live. They were everywhere, in our lullabies, in our great poems and sagas, in our paintings, in the stories told to children. And here we are again, in a time of great danger and encroaching darkness, when the weak are suffering and the strong prey on the rest."

Well, he had me there.

"My father told me that when your father was young, he was not the same man I knew. The Shinar had become warped long before I was born. Before he left for the final battle with the dragon, your father had written your name in the Book of Kings as the Heir, the one who came after him. My father and I and ten others witnessed it."

Yet another thing Dad neglected to mention.

The vampire turned to look at me, its eyes glowing with ruby fire. "That means nothing to me."

Oh.

"You're right. The old kingdom is gone. *Dittalim ushemi.*"

Gone to ash.

"I understand it, and so do my father and my siblings."

"Then why are you here?"

"Because I want my life to matter. I want to be the one who holds back the darkness. I want to dedicate myself to something greater. Every man must have a purpose. I have found my legend. I have found a person who is a beacon of light."

Uh-oh. I needed to put an end to this once and for all.

"Look, I'm not qualified to be a queen or a legend. I don't want to rule. I don't wish to impose my will on anyone. I don't need fame or lullabies with my name attached to them. Right now, I just want to get to where I'm going and rescue a kid from some dickhead who may or may not be a god."

The vampire gave me a big smile.

"What?"

"Asul, the Revered One, the first Sharratum, was the guardian of children. Parents lit incense and fragrant oils in her honor, for when a foreign invader had raided our lands and taken an entire generation of children for their slave pens, she rode into their capital, plunged her sword into their king's heart, and brought the children home."

I groaned.

"Fight against it, rage against it, it doesn't matter. You cannot stop people from following you, no more than you can turn down people who come to you for help. Everything you have done exemplifies the standard to which a queen should aspire, for you are the servant of your people. You help them selflessly without restraint."

"For the last time, I do not have a 'people.'"

"The nephew of a craftsman who is working on your house is taken. You will recover him asking nothing in return, and his family will be loyal to you for all eternity…"

"You are seriously misinterpreting this."

"They will tell stories about you to their children. You will inspire them, so when they see injustice, they will choose to make a stand just as you have done. Try as you might, you cannot change who you are."

"Watch me." Oh, that was a clever comeback. What did I even mean by that? I liked who I was.

The vampire scuttled a few steps ahead and bowed. Cuddles stopped, unsure if she should deliver a stomp to the head.

"I, Rimush, son of Akku and Saile, the Seventh Blade, pledge myself to you, Sharratum. I will serve you in all things, for I have witnessed your deeds and you are worthy of my loyalty."

Great. Just great.

"My family are your eyes, ears, and blades. Call on us in your time of need."

The undead lifted its head, bowed again, and took off down the road back toward the Farm.

Damn it.

[6]

Curran

I leaned on the textured parapet of the front wall. Night had fallen, and the moon was out, big and bright. Behind me, on the other side of the fort, the sea glowed silver, reflecting the moonlight. Here and there the water sparkled when an odd bioluminescent creature rose to the surface, drawn by the stars and the moon.

In front of me our front lawn stretched, a killing zone of three hundred yards, as flat and clear as we could make it. Beyond it the maritime forest rose, a dark wall of stunted live oak, loblolly pine, wax myrtle, and yaupon holly, wedged together, compacted, and pruned by wind and salt into an impenetrable barrier slanted away from the ocean. A road leading to our front gate cut its way through it and vanished in the gloom, where it would eventually join Fort Fisher Boulevard.

The forest was impassable. I had cut several trails through it, but you would need a shapeshifter's nose to find them. When Red Horn came, they would take the road.

Paul's family had gotten in two hours ago, seventeen people

total. Of those, seven were children and five were too elderly to fight. We had put them in the main building with two capable adults to guard the door. The three remaining adults, Paul, his wife, and her brother, came armed with crossbows. They were on the wall now, to my right, waiting. Paul's brother-in-law had also brought a longbow. Not something I'd seen often. It took a particular skill set to draw and fire it correctly. Most people couldn't even sight the target with them because the draw was too strong. They drew and fired in a fraction of a second.

The wind floated in, bringing in a layered mix of scents.

"Dad?" Conlan's voice was barely above a whisper.

"Yes. I can smell them." Shapeshifters. Closing in, moving quietly.

"Is it them?" He sounded a little scared.

"Let's hope not."

I wasn't exactly thrilled about it either. The walls were built to keep out humans, but shapeshifters, even a small group of them, changed things. It wasn't about if I could take them. It was about how many of them would get past me before I did. Conlan wasn't strong enough to stop two or more grown shapeshifters. Not yet.

Another whiff of the breeze, and a familiar scent came through loud and clear. Damn it.

The shapeshifters emerged from the gloom of the forest, running along the road in a column. Seven in total, guarding a human between them. The leader, a short but powerfully built man paused, silhouetted in the moonlight. A ridiculously large sword hung diagonally across his broad back. If he carried it vertically, the damn thing would have dragged along the ground. Of all the people in Wilmington, she found the one guy we'd agreed to avoid at all costs.

The swordsman yanked his sword free and knelt, driving the blade into the packed dirt of the road.

"Hail Beast Lord!" His voice boomed impossibly loud in the quiet night.

Fucking fantastic.

I turned toward Conlan and said very quietly, "Not a word."

Conlan's eyes got really big.

I leaned on the parapet. "Evening, Keelan. Rise and approach."

The last thing I wanted to do was to waste time bellowing back and forth when people were about to attack us.

The shapeshifter group trotted closer. I recognized the human now. Thomas. Where was Kate?

Keelan stopped about ten yards away from the wall. Of the six shapeshifters with him, I knew two. Both had been in their teens when we had separated from the Pack, and, like Keelan, they now stood straight, almost at attention, as if waiting to be inspected. There was a particular look on their faces. I hadn't seen that look for a long time.

"What brings you to this neck of the woods?" I asked.

The werewolf alpha stood up and shrugged. His shoulder muscles rose above his nonexistent neck and drew even with his ears. "Well, my lord. It's like this. We ran into the Consort, and she asked us to see this man safely to your home."

Thomas gave me a little wave.

"Did she now?" She'd waded into something dangerous enough for her to send Thomas here, out of harm's way. Mostly.

What have you walked into, baby?

"Keelan, where did you happen to run into my wife?"

"Oh, nowhere special."

"We were at the Farm," Thomas volunteered.

Fucking hell!

Keelan gave Thomas a reproachful look.

"Why were you at the island stronghold of the People?"

Keelan cleared his throat. "Just a bit of harmless craic with a couple new lads. Sort of an initiation, you could say."

"Not you, Keelan. I really don't want to know what you were doing there. Thomas, why were you and my wife at the Farm?"

Thomas hesitated.

"The man asked you a question," Keelan told him, clearly eager to be off the hot seat.

Thomas took a deep breath and recited in the methodical, calm manner Paul used when he gave us yet another list of absolutely necessary, expensive repairs.

"We went to the Red Horn's headquarters. Your wife asked them who they sold my son to. They told us to 'fuck off.' There was a fight. She won. When the man in charge there, the underboss, wouldn't tell her who took my son, she cut off his head."

So far all of that sounded plausible.

"What happened then? Please be specific."

"She held up the severed head and asked it who bought my son. Then she told the rest of them that since their boss couldn't answer, she would have to keep asking them one by one, until someone told her."

Of course, she had.

"One of them told her that a journeyman named Onyx paid them to kidnap Darin. Onyx works at the Farm."

"And then what happened?

"There were children at the house."

Slavers. This wasn't an isolated incident. They didn't just take one child. They were taking children on a regular basis. Onyx must've hired them because of their experience.

Thomas had gone quiet. The shapeshifters around him froze.

Keelan cleared his throat. "My lord."

He pointed to his eyes.

Oh. I blinked the alpha stare off.

"Continue, please."

"After we got all the kids out of the cages, Kate set the house on fire."

"As she should have," Keelan said.

"What happened after that?"

"We took the children to the Order, so they could be delivered back to their families. The Knight-Protector had her fill out some paperwork and gave her a will-o'-wisp in a cage to take to the man in charge of the People.

"Barrett," Keelan spat the name out like a curse.

Interesting. "Aren't you supposed to be cordial with the People, Keelan?"

"We're both alive. That's cordial enough."

"You don't like him?"

"He likes himself well enough for both of us. All big smiles and sharp knives in your guts, that one."

"Okay, after the Order you went to the Farm?"

Thomas nodded. "We took a boat across. The captain tried to rob us and take the will-o'-wisp."

Of course, he had. "But she killed him?"

"No, he pulled a crossbow on us, but she hit him with some powder, and he shot himself in the foot. Then, a water monster grabbed him and tried to pull him into the water. It had tentacles like a squid or an octopus, but very large, and the weight of it almost capsized the boat."

Keelan nodded sagely. "A kraken, most like."

"A kraken in Cape Fear?" I asked.

"It happens. Probably a wee one chasing fish in from the sea. The juveniles don't have a lot of experience, so they come up the river sometimes."

Good to know.

"Did the kraken eat the man?"

"No. Kate saved him." Thomas sounded like he disapproved.

"How?"

"Well, she said something, a word in a language I didn't understand, and the thing exploded."

A power word. She used a goddamned power word to save the man who tried to rob them. A man who would have shot them if they hadn't complied.

"She became upset and told him to sit still and be quiet. We let him go when we crossed the river."

"The Consort, ever merciful," Keelan opined.

Yes, she was that.

"Did any other unusual things happen on your way to the Farm?"

"No. We got there, she spoke to someone at a desk, and a man came to take her to see Barrett. I waited for her. She was gone for about thirty minutes. She came back and we left the Farm. On the way to the ferry, she told me that Onyx didn't make it, but he told her that he sold Darin to someone named Aaron, who lives on the Emerald Wave and might be a god."

Why not? Why wouldn't it be a child-abducting god? A gang of mundane scumbags or a rogue journeyman would have been too damned easy.

"And that's where the two of you split up and she left you in the company of this gentleman and his friends?"

Keelan spoke up again. "Indeed."

"Was she hurt?"

Keelan grinned. "No. Not at all."

That's all that mattered.

"She also let slip that there might be a bit of trouble here tonight. Unsavory types invading your home. Some of the same cowards who stole Thomas' lad."

His Irish accent was getting thicker. He was plotting something.

"An honest man and his family attacked by brigands," Keelan declared. "Well, we couldn't just stand by and let that kind of thing happen. Could we?"

A chorus of noes answered from the other shapeshifters.

"The Wilmington Pack promised the Consort we'd deliver him here safely, and now we mean to stop here awhile and make sure he stays that way." Keelan paused. "With your permission, of course."

The Wilmington Pack, huh. Oh, Jim was just going to love that. This needed to be handled carefully.

I had no authority to give Keelan permission for anything. Especially here in Wilmington. We'd given up all authority when we'd separated from the Pack. Technically, I wasn't even supposed to be having this conversation.

However, we were a long way from Atlanta, and we could use the extra muscle. Besides, it'd been years since I really gave a fuck what Jim thought about anything. We had been friends once, but that was a long time ago. I'd always known that to Jim only the Pack mattered. It wasn't enough to be a shapeshifter—you had to have the label, so he could put you on the right side of the line between enemy and ally. The moment we left, we became ignorable at best and a potential threat to his leadership at worst. He'd never admit it, but he wanted us gone. It was simpler that way.

We had fought side by side for so long, I had thought that we saw the Pack in the same way. Now I knew we never had. Water under the bridge. Jim had made his choices, and I'd made mine. And Keelan was clearly making his, because he'd been *my-lord*ing me the entire time without any hesitation. For all of his *aw shucks* and "simple Irishman" pretense, Keelan was sharp.

"Are you here in an official capacity, Keelan?"

The werewolf scoffed. "Perish the thought, my lord. Where is it written that a man can't visit a dear friend he's not seen in far too long? Besides, the Consort mentioned you were fixing up this old ruin and told me I should see it for myself."

The Consort and I were going to have a little chat when she got back.

"At night? And with six of your pack in tow? You reckon Jim or Desandra would see it that way?"

"What better time? Besides, we both know I've always been a bit of a Pack floutlaw."

And now he was making words up.

"It's that very same poor attitude that got me shipped up here," Keelan continued. "The advantage is that I can now go weeks or even months without giving much thought to what Jim or the Wolf Queen fancy."

I knew the feeling. And I quite enjoyed it.

Keelan flashed his teeth, and a hint of the alpha shone through. "We were neither of us born with a neck meant for bending. They may exile us, but they can't beat us."

That Kate and I left the Pack voluntarily or that he was, in fact, the alpha of the pack here in Wilmington seemed unimportant to Keelan. Jim had badly miscalculated. I would've made sure Keelan stayed right next to me, where I could keep an eye on him. But Jim and Desandra, those two geniuses, put their heads together and sent him here, on his own, and then they gave him a bunch of promising fighters and potential troublemakers to train. Neither of them had any idea just how much influence Keelan could exert over the Pack. Specifically, over its renders, the cream of the crop when it came to combat.

So I played along. "Banished to this lawless place because we're too fiercely independent?"

"Just so, my lord. The important thing is that we're here now. The two of us and everything's going to be just fine."

Ha! "In that case, welcome, friend Keelan. Bring your people inside. If any of you happen to be hungry, my son will show you where we keep the food. What we have is yours."

"I knew you'd understand. And if the home of my host happened to be attacked while we had our tea, well, we'd be honor-bound to defend it. Who could find fault with that?"

I could think of at least a couple of people. But they were far away from this place and the things that would happen here tonight.

Conlan

When the bad people came, they came like a mob, maybe fifty of them, waving torches and weapons. Grandfather would have called them a horde. But they were like a mob from an old monster movie.

It started with a shapeshifter scout. He slunk out of the woods in warrior form, but it was badly put together and clunky. His jaws didn't fit right, his hind legs were too short, his forelimbs too long, and his pelvis wasn't tilted properly. He was still moving, when he raised his head and inhaled deeply. Suddenly he skidded to a stop.

"One of yours?" Dad asked Mr. Keelan, who stood next to us on the wall.

"Never laid eyes on him. No rats in my crew."

His crew was on the wall too, watching Dad with big eyes. Six shapeshifters, three smelled like wolves, two men and a woman; two were jackals, and they looked like brother and sister; and one was a bouda who reminded me a little of my sister. When we had been talking through the fire and she'd gotten upset about something that had happened to me, her face had been calm and light, but her eyes had been hard. The bouda was like that.

It was the seven shapeshifters and Dad to my left and four archers, Mr. Thomas, Mr. Paul, his wife, and her brother, to my right.

This must be what war would be like. We are under a siege. Like in the stories.

The scout shapeshifter started shaking all over.

"I think he smells you," Mr. Keelan said to Dad.

The wererat turned back the way he'd come and sprinted away. Fast.

"Smart man," Dad said.

"If he is, he'll keep running like the Devil himself is chasing him until he's well out of Wilmington," Mr. Keelan said.

People poured out of the forest tunnel that hugged our road. Ten, fifteen, thirty…fifty…

They approached the walls and stopped about twenty yards away.

"Here they are," Mr. Paul's wife said, her voice sharp with anger.

A woman in the front line started waving her arms. A knot of magic began to form around her.

"Mage," I said. "Front row, third person on the left."

Dad looked at her.

She waved her arms some more.

"It's taking her a while," Mr. Keelan said. "We could just shoot her."

"Let them make the first move," Dad said. "So far, they're just people standing around outside the walls."

Finally, the mage thrust her arms out like she was pushing someone, and a fireball exploded against the wall, three feet to the right of the gates. She had missed. Still, I could feel the heat from where we waited. She wasn't great, but she had some power.

The mob cheered. The man in front, a big, bearded guy painted with red swirls, screamed, "Fuck them up!"

"I believe that's our cue," Dad said. Then he turned and looked directly at me. "Conlan, remember what I said."

"Yes, sir. I stay on the wall. I protect the archers. If I need help, I roar."

Dad nodded and turned away.

"Good lad," Mr. Keelan said. "Keep your wits about you and everything will be fine. Your father and I will handle the rest of this rabble."

Another fireball smashed into the wall, this time less than a foot from the gates.

Dad leaped onto the parapet. Bright moonlight spilled over him, as he stood on the edge, perfectly balanced. Muscles bulged from his shoulders and chest.

"Watch this," Keelan murmured to his shapeshifters. "This is a moment to remember."

When we shifted, it was fast. An instant of pain when you couldn't move, as if you were tied up, then suddenly freedom and a new shape. Dad slowed it down. He did it the way he lifted weights. It wasn't a jerky snap. It was a slow, controlled wave. It began with his head. His skull expanded. Bone flowed like candle wax, the human features melting into a huge, scary lion head. His neck thickened, his shoulders bulged out. His spine stretched, his new body ripping his shirt. Thick muscles wrapped his new arms. Claws burst from his fingers.

The shapeshifters stared at him with glowing eyes, mesmerized.

His hips shifted. His legs grew. Gray fur striped with faint darker stripes slid over his form. His blond hair turned dark and flared into a big, shaggy mane. He opened his giant mouth, showing everyone his terrible fangs, and roared.

THUNDER.

The shapeshifters jerked.

The roar smashed into you. You could feel it in your bones.

THUNDER.

A couple of people down below turned around and started running to the woods.

Mr. Keelan shifted, and a huge black wolf in warrior form landed on the wall. He raised his head, his eyes filled with moonlight, and howled. High and haunting the way only wolves could, singing about the moon, the hunt, and the blood.

The hair on the scruff of my neck stood up.

Down below, the mob took a big step back.

The other shapeshifters changed shape, except for the bouda. The wolves and jackals joined in, turning the howl into a chorus. The bouda giggled in that weird way they did, her cackle jagged like glass breaking.

To the side, Mr. Paul's brother-in-law raised his tall bow and loosed an arrow. It climbed high into the sky, curved, plunged down, and pierced the bearded guy through his head. He fell.

The bouda doubled over laughing.

Dad leaped off the wall. He started the jump in his warrior form, then shifted again in midair. A giant gray lion landed in the middle of the mob. The shock must have been too much because everyone froze. Dad swiped at the nearest fighter with his big paw, sending them flying.

Mr. Keelan held his giant sword up in the air, let out another howl and jumped down. His pack followed except for the bouda who laughed again and moved to stand next to me.

Great. I didn't need a babysitter.

"You can go with them," I told her. "I got this."

She shook her head. "No offence, kid, but your dad and my alpha say otherwise. Sucks for us but at least we get to watch the show."

"My name's Conlan."

"Yeah, I know." She held out her hand with very long, pink nails. "Jynx. With a *y*."

I shook her hand with the long, pink nails.

"Anything happens, stay behind me. If things get really bad, be a good boy and call for backup." She sighed dramatically and pointed down to the ground in front of the gates. "By the look of it, neither of us is going to have any fun tonight."

Below us Dad was crashing into bodies. His huge paws were swatting at everyone in his path, but his claws weren't out. He was holding back.

A man stabbed at him from behind with a spear. Dad twisted, pawed the weapon away, and leaped onto him. His weight forced the man down to the ground. He put the spearman's whole head into his mouth but didn't bite down. He just held it gently and then released him. The man scuttled back, got to his feet, and started running back toward the forest.

"Wow, kid," the bouda gasped. "I thought Keelan's stories were just bullshit, but your dad is a beast!"

Beast lord. Heh.

"Why isn't he killing them though?"

It was obvious. "It's worse," I said.

"What's worse?"

"Living with it. They will remember this, being beaten and mauled. Being so scared that they couldn't even run away. They will never be the same again."

"Killing them is cleaner."

"Some of them are not here by choice. Some of them were forced. There is no way to tell who is who. Those who'll survive get a chance to change their lives and be better. If they don't, we can always kill them later."

She squinted at me. "How old are you again?"

"Eight."

"That's a hard eight, kid. Still, they have the right idea." She nodded at Mr. Paul and his archers, who were shooting into the crowd.

"They are entitled. Those people took Darin, Mr. Paul's nephew. They have a blood claim."

She shook her head at me.

Several feet away from Dad, Mr. Keelan was wading into the crowd swinging his sword back and forth in front of him like it was a giant club. People ran at him, but he was beating them back with the flat side of the blade. His pack was taking down anyone who tried to get behind him.

It was almost over now. They weren't a mob anymore. They were just a herd of people panicking. All of them were scared, some were bleeding badly, and running in every direction to get away from the monsters mauling them. Many were heading back the way they'd come.

A deep bellow tore over the sound of the battle.

At the forest tunnel, trees shuddered, shaking their branches. Something was coming, Something big, moving toward us down the road through the tree tunnel we'd carved out of the woods.

The humans stopped running.

Dad raised his head and looked in that direction.

A stench washed over me. Sour, musky, and wrong somehow.

"That can't be good," Ms. Jynx murmured.

Another bellow. Closer now.

Closer.

The trees shuddered, and a nightmare from old stories stomped out of the forest.

It had to be ten feet tall and held an axe as big as Mr. Keelan's sword over its horned head.

"Holy fuck," Ms. Jynx gasped. "An actual goddamned minotaur!"

No, three minotaurs. Two massive monsters, slightly smaller than the first but with axes of their own, lumbered out to stand next to their leader.

One of the humans ran toward the largest creature, and it cut him in half with one swing of its axe.

"Kill them," it roared. "Kill the cat, kill the dogs, kill the humans behind the walls! Kill them all!"

Dad changed into warrior form and dashed toward the minotaurs.

Grandfather told me about minotaurs. They were not shapeshifters. They were chimeras, and they came from Crete.

A series of deep grunts sounded from behind us.

Ms. Jynx whirled around.

A section of the back wall, the one facing the sea and still under repair, exploded. Stones and mortar came flying toward us, and two big, ugly shapeshifters appeared in the ragged gap. They squeezed into the hole. Jagged, broken portions of the ruined wall tore at their shaggy hides. Wereboars in warrior form. Their eyes were small and red, their tusks huge and yellow.

They forced their way in and paused, pawing the ground with

their hoofed feet, trying to gouge it.

Mr. Paul and his wife turned and fired.

Two arrows sprouted in the larger werehog's chest. The other one looked at them, grunted, and swiped the shafts away with his huge hand.

A layer of muscle, then fat, then quills. The arrows didn't penetrate. They should have penetrated, but they hadn't.

The werehogs sighted the gate. If they opened it, things would get complicated.

The female bouda unsheathed two daggers. "Stay on the wall." She leaped down into the courtyard and landed between the wereboars and the gate.

The wereboars snorted.

My babysitter pointed at the intruders with her daggers. "Hey, piggies! I'm here to carve some bacon off your fat asses."

"Stupid bouda bitch," one of them grunted. "Snuck up behind you. Now we stomp you. Crush your bones. Fuck you. Eat you. Shit you out."

Paul's family shot another two bolts at the boars.

The wereboars snorted some more, ripped the bolts out, and started toward the bouda.

Ms. Jynx flicked her daggers and shifted. A werehyena spilled out, her eyes glowing with ruby fire.

The wereboars charged.

She spun around them like a whirlwind, slicing so fast. Cut, cut, cut, cut…

The wereboars squealed and roared, swiping at her, but she was too quick. Blood flew. The wereboar swung its massive fists at her but couldn't touch her as she darted in and out of its reach.

So, that was how renders fought. *Yeah, I want to do that.*

Ms. Jynx's opponent tried to pull her into a clench, but she ducked and stabbed up into its snout. The wereboar screamed in rage.

She was carving into them, but their wounds closed almost as fast as she cut them. Faster than I healed. Faster than Dad.

The smaller wereboar lunged at her, forcing his way through the barrage of her strikes, trying to lock her into a bear hug, while the other wereboar closed in on her from behind. She had nowhere to go. They smashed into each other, trying to pin her between them. At the last moment, she dropped down into a crouch, and the two boars collided, while she drove her daggers up, into their groins. Stab, stab, stab, so fast.

The wereboars squealed, scrambling. The larger one managed to grab her left arm and yanked her up. She stabbed his thick neck with the other dagger.

He headbutted her.

Oh no.

Ms. Jynx hung off his arm, dazed. He hurled her away. She flew and hit the wall of the keep. Her body made a sound.

The injured wereboar jerked the dagger out of his neck.

Ms. Jynx lay on the ground, by the wall, in a small heap. She wasn't moving.

"Conlan," Mr. Paul said. "It's time to ask for help."

I glanced over my shoulder. Dad and the biggest minotaur were ripping into each other. If I called him, he wouldn't get here in time, and the minotaur would kill someone.

I looked back at the courtyard. The two werehogs started toward Ms. Jynx, their sharp, heavy hooves stomping. They were ready to gore her.

No.

These people came here to hurt us. They took Jason's brother. They tried to hurt Mom. They attacked our home, they fought my dad, and now they were about to kill my friend. I wasn't going to run, and I wasn't going to hide behind my father. And I wouldn't allow them to hurt anyone.

"Stop," I ordered.

Two shaggy monster heads swiveled toward me.

"What are you going to do, little man?" the smaller wereboar demanded. The other snorted.

I jumped.

I weighed about 60 pounds in my human body. But I weighed 4 times as much in the warrior form.

The wereboar saw me change in mid-air and threw himself to the side. I'd wanted to land on top of him. Instead, I only caught him with my hind foot. My claws ripped through his thick hide, and he squealed in surprise.

I bounced clear, putting myself between them and Ms. Jynx.

The boars stared at me.

I snarled at them. It wasn't a call for help. It was a challenge. I wasn't as big as my dad, but I was six feet tall, my claws and teeth were sharp, and I was also a lion. Lions ate boars.

Ms. Jynx jumped up. "You dummy!"

Oh. She'd been pretending.

The bouda cackled next to me. I stood up straight.

The wereboars scoured the ground, digging at it with their hooves.

We moved at the same time. The two wereboars attacked. Ms. Jynx shot forward, and I shot backward, bounced up off the wall, picking up height, and launched myself at them. The larger wereboar screamed as we collided and went down, both of us biting and clawing. We rolled around on the ground of the courtyard, tearing into each other.

He was so strong. I wasn't going to outmuscle him. But he was big and slow. I remembered my training and decided to switch tactics. I bit his ear. Hot, angry magic sliced my tongue. Ow. I bit down harder. The wereboar squealed, flailed, and I broke free of him.

I rolled to my feet, spat the nasty ear out, and gestured for him to come at me.

The enraged boar charged, and at the last moment I leaped straight up.

Before he could stop, I jumped on his back. I dug all of my

claws into him and bit down hard on his neck. Just below the base of his skull.

He tried to shake me off. He threw himself onto the ground, trying to crush me beneath his bulk.

I felt some of my ribs snap. Ouch, it hurt. It hurt!

But I had him now, and I wasn't letting go.

He thrashed about, panicked now and losing lots of blood. I could feel him getting weaker.

With my teeth still buried in his foul-tasting flesh, I shifted my head more into a lion's. My teeth got bigger. Slowly I could feel the boar's muscles tearing and giving away. I put as much pressure as I could on the bones of his neck. I bit down until my jaw ached, trying to crush his throat.

It lasted forever.

His neck crunched.

He spasmed in his death throes, his huge body crushing me.

Suddenly my teeth were free.

His head rolled on his shoulders, hanging on by bits of skin and ruined muscle.

Not yet. It's not done yet.

I bit through the rest of the neck and pulled the head free.

His dead eyes stared back at me.

I did it!

I kicked free of the body, jumped to my feet, held the head up, and roared louder and longer than I ever had.

The body of my enemy lay at my feet, and I was alive. And strong. Stronger than him. Stronger than anybody.

"Son," Dad's voice seemed very far away. "That's damned impressive but what happened to calling for help?"

Oh. I managed to make my mouth work. "Hey, Dad."

He was standing just a few feet away, human again and holding the head of the largest minotaur.

Nearby, Ms. Jynx, still in warrior form, leaned on Mr. Keelan. He was speaking softly to her and patting her shoulder. She was covered in blood, little of it hers, and laughing hysterically. She couldn't seem to stop.

"You seemed busy," I told Dad and changed back into human form.

"I was a bit." He hefted the enormous head into his hands.

Mr. Keelan turned toward us and was looking at me and Dad with a strange expression.

"My lord," he said. "Don't be too hard on the lad. He fought a hell of a fight against a larger, more experienced foe. Remind you of anyone?"

"Don't start, Keelan. If his mother finds out about this"—Dad used the minotaur's horns to point at the bodies of the wereboars—"what happened here tonight will seem like a pleasant dream. I mean it."

He looked around at everyone else, his eyes a bright, furious gold. "Nobody says a word about this to Kate. Am I clear?"

Everybody said *yes* at the same time.

Dad turned back to me. "Right now, I need to go and find your mom. I'm sure she's fine. The guy on the ship is probably not a god but you never know. Conlan, I'm very proud of you. Let's keep the part about you, her beloved eight-year-old son, killing a giant wereboar and waving its head around, to ourselves. This will be our little secret. This is a shapeshifter thing, and your mom doesn't always understand shapeshifter things."

He dropped the minotaur head on the ground.

"I promise," I told him. Mom loved us, but she also worried a lot.

Mr. Keelan cleared his throat. "If I might make a small suggestion. Troy is a decent medmage. Perhaps it would be good to have him along with you?"

The male jackal spoke up. "I trained under Doolittle. I'm certified to treat shapeshifters and humans."

"That's good enough for me," Dad told him. "I'd be happy to have you come with."

Dad turned to me again and paused. "Conlan, you're in charge until we get back. You've earned it."

Dad said I earned it. I stood up straighter.

His eyes flashed gold. "But if Keelan stays a bit, listen to what he has to say."

"You go and find the Consort, my lord. The boy and I will take care of everything here. Nothing to worry about."

As I watched Dad and Troy break into a run heading down the road, Mr. Keelan clamped his big hand on my shoulder. "Nothing better than a good fight before breakfast. Still, perhaps we could start by tidying up a bit, eh? We wouldn't want your mother coming home to a messy house, would we?"

Ms. Jynx exhaled and finally stopped shaking.

"Got a hold of yourself?" Keelan asked.

She nodded. "What I want to know is where the hell did they get the fucking minotaurs?"

"From the Labyrinth," Troy's sister said.

"Duh!" Ms. Jynx said. "Seriously, Helen?"

"No, I mean it. For real. Troy and I are Greek. Our uncle knows a lot of people in our community, so when we got stationed here by the Pack, we went to pay our respects. They warned us about the minotaurs. There is the Labyrinth in Crete. It's a magic space like Unicorn Lane. The minotaurs live there. They are always male, so they have to kidnap women to reproduce."

That was pretty much what Grandfather had said.

"They're territorial and they have disputes with each other," Ms. Helen said. "These three were a father and his sons. They were forced out, so they boarded the first ship they could find and ended up here two years ago. They destroyed the local gangs and built their own."

Mr. Keelan's eyes went green. "And you kept it to yourself?"

The werejackal raised her hands. "It never came up?"

"Helen, for future reference, this is the kind of information I need to have as your alpha. Do we understand each other?"

She nodded. "Yes, Alpha."

"Good. Let's go clean up."

"Okay, I get the minotaurs, but what about the pigs?" Ms. Jynx asked.

"Clean up, Jynx," Mr. Keelan said. "You've met the Consort before. Focus on what's important."

IT TOOK AN HOUR TO GET ALL THE CORPSES AND BODY PARTS INTO A pile. It took longer for them to burn in the bonfire. I even had to feed some of my magic into it to get it hot enough. Once it got going the smell and the smoke were awful.

When we were done, Mr. Keelan took my wereboar's head and placed it on the ground in front of the fire. Right next to the head of the largest minotaur.

"Well, that's the last of them." Then he stood back and just looked at them for a while. "Great big bastards, weren't they? I don't know about the minotaurs, but the two hogs smelled like wereboars to me. Usually, shapeshifters turn back to human after death but not these pigs."

"They were cursed," I said.

Mr. Keelan raised his eyebrows at me.

Ms. Jynx ran over to us. "Good news! I figured out the pigs! They are—"

"Cursed," Mr. Keelan said.

She blinked at him. "How did you know?"

He nodded at me.

"I tasted the magic when I bit off his ear," I explained. "It was witch magic. Very strong."

"Are you going to be okay?" Mr. Keelan asked. "Do we need to purify you somehow?"

My grandmother had been a witch and Mom was one too, when she needed it. I knew how to protect myself, but it didn't matter, because the curse was very specific. "I'll be fine."

"Well, anyway," Ms. Jynx said. "I had a chat with that fire mage. She took an arrow in the knee, and she doesn't deal with pain well, so she was very cooperative. Apparently, the two were-hogs are local boys, Buck and Grady. They are—were—first-grade assholes. They did home invasions, collected gambling debts, assaulted people, your low-level muscle shit. Somehow, they got the bright idea to break into a house of a powerful local witch. They went in human and came out as that. Apparently, she told them that since they lived their lives like pigs, she would make their outside match their inside. So yeah. They didn't turn back because they couldn't. They are permanently stuck like that."

They were. It was over now.

"Good work," Mr. Keelan told Ms. Jynx.

She grinned at him and walked away.

Mr. Keelan studied the heads some more. "Looks like you've got the best trophy of the night."

"No, sir. The one my dad killed is bigger than mine."

Mr. Keelan scoffed. "Nonsense, lad. You're young yet, you lack a proper sense of proportion. That porcine shithead was twice your size. How did it feel?"

"At first I was scared," I admitted.

"Anyone would be. Wereboars are as tough as they are stupid. Even the bears don't like fighting them. After you were afraid, what then?"

"I was mad."

"Why?"

"They broke into our home. They wanted to hurt Ms. Jynx. And this one called me 'little man.'"

"His mistake. Look at him, he's not bigger than you now, is he?"

"No, sir. He's just dead."

"How did it feel to tear that ugly head off his hairy shoulders?"

I'd been exhausted and beat up but honestly, it felt...

"It was amazing," I told him.

"Aye, it was that. But your father's got the right of it. It's a shame your mother will never know how brave you were, but this is shapeshifter business." Mr. Keelan sighed, "Best not to trouble your mother with the details." He paused. "Still, even if you and your father never speak of it again, it doesn't matter. Do you know why?"

"No."

"Because I saw it. We all did. My people. The humans. All of us."

"So?" Why did that matter? I was tired and hungry and wished he'd just get to the point.

He seemed very serious now, like it was important that I understood what he was trying to tell me. It was a little like speaking to Grandfather.

"So, that's how legends begin, lad. People who were here will tell the story to them that wasn't. And those people will spread the tale."

"Of how you and Dad killed three minotaurs? Nobody will believe it. It's too crazy."

Mr. Keelan shook his head. "No, lad. The story of how the Beast Lord's son, when he was just a small boy, beheaded a magical wereboar with his bare hands. That's the important bit. That's the part people will remember."

We were alone, but his voice was barely above a whisper.

I frowned. "He's not the Beast Lord. Not anymore."

Mr. Keelan rubbed his hands together and smiled again. "Is he not? My mistake. No matter. What if we go inside and find something to eat. I don't know about you, but I'm fucking starving."

[7]

Kate

The Emerald Wave was an enormous ship. The sheer size of it was insane. It had to be about 1,000 feet long, and from my spot on Siren Call Road, I could see nine decks still rising above water. The windows of the third and fourth deck glowed with pale feylantern light from within. The massive cruise ship had run aground about twelve hundred feet offshore. A long rickety-looking pier connected her to the beach, and the whole thing looked absurd, like a whale, caught on a tiny fishing line, being pulled out of the ocean against her will.

According to Thomas, the Emerald Wave had gone off course during a particularly nasty storm decades ago and become lodged in a sand bank. The Coast Guard had tried to pry it lose with tugboats and gotten nowhere. In addition, something had attacked the ship during the magic wave that had killed all its instruments, and two of its compartments had filled with water, flooding the engine room.

Refloating the ship was a complicated process involving draining the fuel tanks while simultaneously pumping in salt water to keep it upright, and the cost of getting the Emerald Wave up and running again would have been astronomical, so the cruise line had left it where it was. It had been looted, stripped, and finally abandoned, and now it supposedly housed a cult.

"Look at that evil lair, Cuddles. No ziggurats, no ritualistic poles with skulls on them, no giant faces carved anywhere or big metal fire braziers. These modern evil god followers just don't care to put in the work."

Cuddles remained unimpressed. But then again, a big derelict ship was scary enough. I certainly didn't want to go in there.

I nudged Cuddles, and she reluctantly walked to the pier.

Aaron didn't seem to be doing any of the usual things people connected to gods did. But Onyx was well trained and educated. He would've recognized divinity, so there was some sort of deity attached to all this. How and in what capacity remained to be seen.

Water gods and their followers were never fun. Gods in general weren't fun. They were fed by faith and shaped by the beliefs of their followers. If a god was poorly known or too obscure, they couldn't scrape together enough power to manifest. The leading theory said that they didn't even exist until their followers' belief achieved a certain critical mass. One of the articles I'd read recently had somehow brought quantum physics into it, which went right over my head.

If a god was too well known, they couldn't manifest either. Everyone's Jesus and Buddha looked different, and the conflicting ideas canceled each other out. The holy people of the larger religions packed a lot of power, however.

That left a lot of mid-sized gods, who were famous enough but not worshipped too widely. Specificity helped, and "functional" gods got the first dibs on followers. Few neopagans prayed to Zeus aside from the annual rites. A lot more people prayed to Eileithyia and with a greater passion, even though some of them had no idea who she was until they were about to become parents.

Chances of being struck by lightning were low, but dying in childbirth or losing a baby to some sickness was a real possibility.

If a water god appeared, they were likely in charge of a specific body of water, like a river or a lake, or performing a specific function like Satet, who oversaw the Nile's floods. Yet here we were, heading toward the ocean. Encountering someone like Poseidon should have been highly unlikely, but it wasn't impossible.

It might not even be a water god. It could be an animal god that lived in the ocean, although animal gods had yet to demonstrate the ability to speak. I'd run across a few—and Curran had eaten several of them—and all of them were more on the level of abnormally powerful magic animals rather than true deities.

It was pointless to try to figure it out. I simply didn't have enough data.

We reached the pier. I looped Cuddles' reins on the rail and tied a run-away knot. If things got scary, and she jerked her head, the reins would come free. Having a horse or a mammoth jenny wander about with several feet of reins dangling over them would be a recipe for a broken leg or some other disaster, but it was still better than getting eaten outright.

"If shit hits the fan, take off like a rocket."

Cuddles ignored me.

I stepped onto the pier. It held against all expectations, and I started walking. The ocean spread on both sides of me, teeming with life. A lot of that life glowed softly with a rainbow of colors.

Too much glowing. Especially around the ship. In fact, entirely too much marine life altogether. The waters by our fort weren't nearly so crowded. Not a good sign.

I cleared the pier. A metal gangway, slightly rusted and crusty with salt, was attached to the side of the ship, leading up to the first intact deck at a sharp angle. It was barely wide enough for one person. Okay.

I climbed the gangway. It didn't collapse. Thank Fate for small favors.

A school of fish, pulsing with green, darted below me through the water, narrowly avoiding a jellyfish as big as a tire shimmering lemon-yellow and sparkling with magenta. Yep, definitely not a normal ocean. The ship was a magical nexus of some sort.

I climbed to the deck and almost collided with a heavy-set man carrying a big club.

"What do you want?"

"I'm here to see Aaron."

"The fuck you are!"

He swung the club. I swept his legs out from under him and shoved him left. He made a lovely splash.

Ahead a wooden double door stood open. It seemed out of place on the ship. They must've retrofitted it. I went through it, into a short, arched hallway, and came out into a large space.

I wasn't sure what I expected, but this wasn't it. It looked like the inside of a mall. Exactly like the inside of a mall. A long passageway stretched to both sides, with a curved storefront with golden letters spelling out *GUEST SERVICES* directly in front of me. Shops and cafés lined the walls. A Starbucks, a karaoke bar, some kind of Italian restaurant. Most of it had been abandoned and stripped down to the bone. The air smelled of salt and bacon.

On the right the passage was dark. On the left, feylanterns illuminated what looked like a plaza. *Left it is.*

I strolled along the storefronts. The plaza lay ahead, a well-lit round space with ten tables, a restaurant manned by a woman who was cooking bacon, and a bathroom at the opposite end. Six of the tables were occupied. Fourteen people total, some eating, some playing cards, wearing normal street clothes. It was close to midnight. The acolytes of Aaron were night owls.

One of the benefits of being married to a shapeshifter and having a shapeshifter son was that I'd learned to move very quietly. I was right on top of the nearest occupied table before a young woman sitting at it looked up and jerked back.

Everyone looked at me. None of them seemed to be packing a

lot of magic power. Most of them didn't look well fed, and there was a lot of apprehension in their eyes. Small fry followers. Followers were good at taking orders.

"One of you is supposed to take me to Aaron," I told them.

"Umm," an older man said. "Why?"

I gave him a hard stare. "Who are you that you're asking me about my private business?"

"Nobody," the woman next to him said. "He's a nobody. I'll take you."

She got up. "This way."

We left the plaza, walked along the mall hallway some more, and then took stairs down. One deck, two, three...We had to be below sea level or close to it.

"So is it true that Aaron is a god?" I asked.

"He isn't a god," the older woman said quietly. "But he has god powers."

"How did he get them?"

The older woman didn't respond.

There were only three ways to get god powers. You were born with them, which made you an avatar or some variation thereof, you were granted them as a reward, or you bargained for them. Technically, you could merge with them or devour them, but that almost never happened. Almost.

An avatar wouldn't have to rely on gangs to steal people for him. He would be powerful enough to take what he wanted. The reward was equally unlikely. There were no signs of any gods around us. A god who was rewarding a follower would want their name glorified and their symbols displayed. That left only the third possibility. A bargain had been struck. Probably under duress of some sort.

Another formerly luxurious hallway. Doors stood open on both sides. They looked like luxury dining rooms or maybe casino rooms converted into kitchens or possibly laboratories. Long metal tables everywhere.

A hint of magic pulled on me. I went through the doorway on the right, following it.

A large tank sat against the wall, glowing bright enough to light up the whole room and emanating faint magic. An assortment of feylantern glass lay on the tables next to it: globes, tubes, and bunches of small spheres. Some sort of bioluminescent algae, but magically charged. I was wondering why the feylanterns here were so bright. Normally they were glass vessels filled with magically charged air, but here they were filled with water and that algae.

"How long do they last?" I asked.

The woman had stopped in the doorway of the lab. "About a year."

"You sell these?"

She nodded. "Garvey does."

"Who is Garvey?"

"The CFO."

Interesting cult they had.

I moved to the next table. A big plastic bin filled with pearls of all sizes and colors. Golden, white, pink, purple, black…They came in a variety of shapes. Some were oval, some were round, others had ridges. A few were teardrops. A small fortune.

I glanced at her.

"The kids get these," she said. "When Garvey can convince Aaron to let a couple of them forage on the ocean floor. Aaron hates it, but Garvey says we need the money."

She didn't sound happy about it. Her eyes were haunted, too.

I moved to the next table. Slow cookers. Four of them. Wrapped in chains, padlocked, and secured to metal rings bolted to the floor. And warded. Good wards, too. Hmm.

"What's in these?"

The woman's face jerked.

"Who set these wards?"

"Aaron," she said barely above a whisper.

Aaron clearly knew what he was doing.

I walked over to the large trashcan with a sealed lid, unlocked the latch, and looked inside. Chunks of a glass sponge, bright yellow when it was in the water, and now dull.

Oh.

"Who has Huntington's?" I asked.

She took a deep breath. "My daughter. She's only 16."

Back when Curran and I had run the Mercenary Guild in Atlanta, one of the mercs, a veteran, had a son who had developed the symptoms of Huntington's disease. Certain types of glass sponges contained magically potent bacteria that slowed the progression of disease and sometimes stopped it completely. The extraction process was complex and incredibly expensive. These sponges only grew in cold, deep water. We had gotten ours from Canada.

The slow cookers were bacteria vats, fed and protected by the wards.

"Is this why you're here?"

She started crying. I let her sob. There was nothing to be said. She was here for her daughter, she knew it was wrong, it ripped her apart, but still she stayed because she couldn't let her daughter die. She was desperate and trapped. That didn't excuse anything she had done.

"And the others?" I asked.

"It's just four families," she managed. "Us, the Allens, the Lipnicks, and the Rios. Rodney Allens' wife has MS, Denis Lipnick has Huntington's, and..."

"I get it," I told her.

"They give us medicine every month. Just enough."

Cults exploited people, and those who got sucked in, especially on the bottom layer of the hierarchy, weren't usually bad people. They were looking for something better, a little bit of hope, or a way to deal with overwhelming things in their life. Instead, they ended up as free labor, brainwashed and used, their vulnerabilities and fears molded into a leash that held them in place.

There was no better leash than saving the life of someone you loved. It made people do terrible things.

"Let's go," I told her.

We crossed the length of the hallway and came to a metal bulkhead door that looked newer than the walls around it. The woman cranked the wheel, strained, and swung the door open. In front of us a narrow metal bridge spanned a flooded space four feet above the sea. The water glowed with blues and yellows, lit up by a school of tiny jellyfish. Under the jellyfish, about six or seven feet down, something slithered. It was long and sinuous, thicker than me and butter-yellow. I couldn't tell if it was a mass of tentacles, some prehistoric marine worm, or a knot of giant underwater snakes. It had no eyes or mouth. Just length.

The woman swallowed and started across the metal bridge, taking tiny little steps.

The thing under the water kept sliding, moving and twisting slowly. It filled the entire floor of the chamber, wall to wall.

Another hesitant step. Another.

"Stop," I told her.

She froze, clutching at the rails.

"How much further?"

"Through that door and straight down that hallway. We are not allowed to go past the red archway."

"Come back."

She backed up, covering the three feet of bridge separating her from me in a flash.

"If I were you, I would go and get the other families and then I would look for something I could use to cut metal chains."

She stared at me, her face blank.

"The wards on those vats are direct-line wards. They will disappear when Aaron dies. I would get those cutters ready and wait by the vats until the wards disappeared."

Her eyes went wide.

"Then I would take these vats and hop a leyline to Atlanta. I would take them to Biohazard and give them to Luther Dillon, and I would tell him that Kate sent me."

She stared at me.

"It's not for you. You know what you are. It's for your daughter. Deputy Director Luther Dillon. Go."

She took off back the way we came at a near run.

I once had done a horrible thing to save Julie's life. It had gone against everything I stood for, and I'd still done it. I had watched her in a coma as she had lain there, dying second by second. Fading. It had been a kind of madness where nothing except saving her mattered.

I started across the metal bridge, moving lightly on my toes. The slithering thing shifted slowly below. To come all this way and then get eaten by an overgrown ocean tapeworm wasn't part of the plan.

Where did they get cold water sponges? You had to get them fresh.

The bridge ended. I stepped onto the metal platform at the end, opened another bulkhead door, and stepped into a hallway. It was long, with an eighteen-foot ceiling. Above me hundreds of glass or crystal planks hung from the ceiling like a constellation of icicles, reflecting the bluish light coming from the clusters of feylanterns on the walls. The effect was a bit eerie.

Ahead a red arch cut the hallway in half. It was shiny and thick, and while it might have fit in with the décor before, now it felt jarring and ominous.

I came within two feet of it and stopped. A ward. And a good one, too.

Wards served two purposes, to protect and contain, and they operated by changing the balance of the elements in the environment. Each ward was a magic field, defined by anchors. The sets of anchors were nearly infinite. There were the classic 4 elements:

fire, water, earth, and air, or the equally classic 5 elements: wood, fire, earth, metal, and water. You could use chemical substances, fires burning different fuels, light sources in a specific pattern, or bodily fluids. If I really needed an impenetrable ward, I would use my blood as an anchor. Precision and balance were key.

This ward felt even and solid as a wall. Expertly set, with the anchor placement perfectly calculated. This took training, math, geometry, and deep understanding of the environment. I couldn't see the anchors, which probably meant the ward mage had embedded them in the arch on the other side. Smart.

I could try to break it, but the backlash could be severe, and shooting myself in the foot just before the fight wasn't the best strategy. Neither was announcing my power level this early or spending that much magic.

We were in an aquatic environment. Water was notoriously difficult to work with when it came to wards, because it never stayed the same. It flowed, it evaporated, it absorbed things. Sometimes things grew in it. Wards depended on the consistency of the anchors.

The best ward here would be either fire-based, because it was a drastic change, or element-neutral, something like runes. It was tried, true, and reliable, with a precise power value. Chemical substances or botanicals would degrade in the damp environment, and fire would be hard to maintain.

No, it would be runes. Probably Elder Futhark, the oldest available.

Every Elder Futhark ward would contain Elhaz, the rune of defense. Everything else reinforced it. Number 9, thrice three, was sacred to Old Germanic people, and the best rune wards included 9 runes.

I'd stick Elhaz in the middle of that arch and follow it with a pair of Eihwaz, the *Yew Tree*, on each side for magic amplification. Then, I'd put Inguz, a *Fertility* rune, on each side. It protected one's household. This was his house; he'd be a fool not to use it.

That gave me 5 runes. The other four would be there for pure power. A pair of Thurisaz, *Thorn,* runes was a safe bet, defense against unexpected attacks and adversaries, a good magic generator. But he would need to channel all that magic toward Elhaz, which meant he had to use something with a drive.

Let's see, Ehwaz, *Horse,* Fehu, *Cattle,* or Uruz, *Wild Ox,* would all give him the flow he needed. Uruz was too unpredictable and mostly used for explosive power. *Horses* were okay, but *Cattle* would give me steady flow without any surprises. I'd put them on the very bottom of the arch to create two currents of magic that would surge upward through all the runes, getting stronger and more refined until they met in Elhaz at the top of the arch.

I pulled a vial of sulfuric acid from a pouch on my belt. I only had enough acid for a couple of runes. Here was to hoping it worked.

I drip-drew Raidho, *Wagon,* which looked like a clunky *R* on the metal floor, right at the point where the invisible wall of the ward blocked the hallway. I followed it with a simple *I,* Isa for *Ice.* The metal smoked with toxic fumes. Ugh.

I dripped the last few drops onto the bottom of the *R* and waited.

The acid ate at the floor, creeping toward the ward. Three, two…

Magic popped like a firecracker. The runes on the floor sparked white, the ward flashed silver, and for a second a solid wall of magic, like a thin barrier of translucent ice, formed within the arch.

The wall cracked and broke, melting into nothing.

Ha-ha. I'd hitched his cattle to a wagon and froze it. Right now the owner of the ward would be doubled over with one hell of a headache.

Magic swirled around, a mix of thick, potent currents, flowing from the hallway ahead. The ward had blocked them, but now they splashed all around me, volatile, chaotic, twisting into eddies and whirlpools.

This was a nexus, a hole in the fabric of the world that bled magic. Atlanta had one too, a lot larger than this one. They called it Unicorn Lane, a place where metal rubble sprouted fangs, corrosive moss grew on power lines, and everything tried to eat you.

This explained the abnormal concentration of marine life.

I stepped through the arch and turned around. Yep, Elder Futhark runes, embedded in the arch. He'd used *Horses* instead of *Cattle,* but my frozen wagon still worked. The runes themselves had been etched into the bone and stained with metal. Not silver —the hue was wrong, and it wasn't smooth, it was geometric and soldered on there. An osmium alloy of some sort. Very expensive. Very rare.

Damn it.

Well, it changed nothing.

Thomas should've gone to the Order with his petition. If I survived this little adventure, the next time we met, I'd tell Claudia all about it.

I turned and marched down the hallway toward the light.

I WENT THROUGH ANOTHER RED ARCH—UNWARDED THIS TIME—AND paused in its shadow, just before the doorway. The hallway opened into a large room, lit up with clusters of feylanterns arranged into eight-rayed, layered snowflakes on the ceiling. The light was so bright, it looked like the middle of the day, and I stayed just on the edge of it.

This must've been a nightclub or some sort of concert venue with a dance floor and a raised stage at the far end of the room. The dance floor was now in front of me, the floor itself made of plastic or glass tiles, transparent and shimmering with embedded glitter. The ocean had flooded the section of the ship below this room. I could see the salt water under my feet.

On the left, a stairway led to a balcony that curved along the room, filled with tables and padded chairs. On the right, a massive, ragged hole gaped in the hull, big enough to drive a semi through sideways. It had carved off a chunk of the ship all the way to the bottom. The sea was just below the floor, and whatever lay on the other side of that hole wasn't the Figure Eight beach. In fact, it wasn't even America's Atlantic coast.

Huge crags jutted from the waters in the distance. The same rocky boulders continued under water, stretching to the ship in stone reefs. Jewel-colored anemones sheathed the stone, glowing with yellow-green, orange, electric blue, and neon pink among patches of dark mussels. Mollusks, sea slugs in every color of the rainbow, and ringed jellyfish flashing with bright lights swam and hovered among the reefs. A huge brown skate glided by, slipped under the glass tiles, backlit by the reef, and floated right under my feet. The magic was so thick, you could cut it with a knife and spread it on bread.

Most of North Carolina's coastal bottom was sand. There were artificial reefs and oyster sanctuaries, built pre-Shift, but none of them were here, in this spot. And those cliffs in the distance looked like something from Oregon or Washington... Except there were no trees. The Pacific Northwest was heavily wooded along the coast, and I couldn't see a single tree.

Thomas' source was right. The Emerald Wave did have a hole that could only be seen from the inside.

This was a tear in the fabric of reality, and I had no idea where it led. A pocket realm, built by some cosmically powerful being? A portal leading somewhere else? None of the options were good.

More importantly, maintaining this hole would require a ton of magic. Usually you saw these junctions in place of wild, very concentrated magic, because their creators used the environmental magic to power them. This didn't feel like that. It felt like there was a definite focal point, some kind of magic generator right off the ship, that kept this portal going.

I leaned a bit to the right, trying to get a better view of the room.

Nine people sat on the floor by the far end of the hole, huddled together, each of them chained by their ankle. Three adults: a skinny woman in her thirties with scars on her pale arms and defiant eyes; a man about Thomas' age, gaunt and beaten down, his hair a dark curtain over his bronze face; and a young woman, barely in her twenties, with bright red gills that stood out against the dark brown skin of her throat. The rest were children, all sizes and ages. The youngest looked about ten.

The chains stretched into the hole and vanished into the water.

Okay. Haven't seen that before.

As I watched, the gaunt man leaned forward, and I saw the boy behind him. Darin. Alive. Wet and looking desperate, but alive.

I looked past the prisoners to the four-foot-high stage, where a big golden throne rose in the center, shaped like some mutant conch shell and gilded. Where did they even find that thing? It looked like a prop pulled out of some over-the-top opera.

A man in his thirties sat on the throne. Tan, with light brown hair, he slumped forward, his elbow on the armrest, his forehead resting on his hand. He wore a blue linen robe, and his feet were bare.

Hello, Aaron. Got you out of bed there, buddy, with my ward breaking? So sorry. No worries, I'm coming to help you with that migraine.

Next to the throne, a much older man hovered, anxiously rubbing his bony, weather-browned hands. His wispy white hair hung limp over the back of his neck. He wore a wrinkled garment that might have been a chasuble with the Catholic embroidery replaced by an appliqué patch with wave symbols on it.

A teenage girl sat on the stage, dangling her feet off it. Thin and dark-haired, with an odd bluish tint to her pale skin, she wore a tank top and a pair of shorts. She couldn't have been older than 16. Her stomach was bloated. I would've guessed she was pregnant, but the shape didn't look quite right. She looked...lumpy.

Behind the throne, on the wall, a two-foot-long white feather hung off two chains. Brown splashes stained the white barbs. Dried blood.

White feather, freaky ocean, cold water sponges that only grew in the depths, cliffs...

Oh, you dumb fuck.

I walked out into the open.

A thin female prisoner saw me first and elbowed the man next to her. The lot of them stared at me. On the left, a boy about Conlan's age walked through a small doorway, carrying a platter with a pill bottle and a glass of water on it. He noticed me and froze.

The teenage girl saw me. A shiver ran through her. She hopped off the stage and bounced in place, whining in a high-pitched voice, like a toddler on the edge of a tantrum. "Mine, mine, mine, mine..."

The man on the throne waved his hand at her without bothering to look up.

She grinned. Her smile stretched from ear to ear, literally. Her head split, and the top half of it went up, her mouth wet and red, lined with conical teeth. Her thick, pink tongue wiggled in the sea of teeth like some weird worm. She was like a Muppet from an ancient kids' show, except this wasn't cute, it was horrifying.

She slammed her jaw shut, her teeth making a loud, bone-scraping click, and charged me.

I unsheathed my sword.

She was hellishly fast.

I dodged, and she swiped at me with her hands, each finger tipped with a sharp, blue claw. I backed away, blocking her swipes with Sarrat. Her claws rang on the metal, like pebbles flicked at the blade. She caught my left forearm and gripped it, throwing her weight into it. Her mouth gaped open, and she tried to pull me forward, toward her snapping teeth.

I rammed the pommel of Sarrat into her temple.

The blow knocked her back. She stumbled to the side, her eyes wild, and I took a step and kicked her in that bulging stomach. The front kick took her off her feet. She flew a couple of yards backward, fell, and vomited up an undigested human forearm, the hand still attached. A very small hand.

"Kill her!" the female prisoner with the angry eyes screeched. "She eats children!"

The thing on the floor grabbed the arm and stuffed it back into her mouth. Her neck expanded, she gulped it down, and then I was on her. She'd managed to come up from the crouch in time to meet me straight-on. Sarrat's blade slid into her chest with a soft whisper and cut into her heart.

Her pale blue eyes stared at me, shocked.

I twisted the sword in her heart, ripping it, and withdrew.

She whimpered, "Mine..." and collapsed on the floor.

I stabbed her through the left eye, driving Sarrat into her brain in case she decided to regenerate, freed the sword with a sharp tug, and looked at the man on the throne. "Cute opening act. Can't wait to see the headliner."

THE OLD MAN PEERED AT ME WITH WATERY EYES, ANXIOUSLY rubbing his hands. The man on the throne looked up, his face slack with annoyance. He looked to be somewhere around 30, maybe 35. He had the worn-out complexion of a naturally pale person who'd gone through too many sunburns, with tired skin creased by premature lines. Stubble hugged his jaw, the result of neglect and apathy. His light brown eyes, however, were sharp.

I glanced at the child with the platter. "What's your name?"

"Boy," he said.

Great. "Is that what he calls you?"

The child ducked his head.

"What was your name before you were here?"

"Antonio."

"Good to meet you, Antonio. I want you to cross the room and sit down with those people over there." I nodded at the chained-up group. I needed to get all of the people I had to protect into a single clump.

The boy scurried behind me to the group and sat down next to Darin. Thomas' son was watching me. They were all watching me. I needed to chat Aaron up to confirm exactly what god I was dealing with. The white feather was pretty clear, but verifying never hurt.

"Love what you've done with the place, Aaron," I said. I kept my tone conversational. Having him lash out randomly wasn't the plan. "And this must be Garvey?"

The old man gave me a startled look.

"You broke my ward," Aaron said.

"Yes."

"How?"

"Hitched your cows to an iced wagon."

He thought about it and grimaced. The mother of all headaches raging in his skull was making it hard to think.

His voice was tired. "Did Claudia send you?"

"No, but I'll let her know I dropped by the next time I see her."

"Are you a knight?"

"No. Who was the girl?"

"A pet. What do you want?"

I pointed to the chained-up people. "You're a slaver and a human trafficker. When you sink that low, you have to expect a reckoning."

He didn't say anything.

"I was hoping for a hint of shame or regret," I said. "This is very disappointing."

"A mercenary," he finally said, as if the word was slimy. "How much did they pay you?"

"I'm doing this pro-bono."

"Why?"

"Because you've become a problem I decided to resolve."

"Did I now?"

"Looks that way."

"Do you even know who I am?"

"I can make an educated guess. You were a knight-enchanter. Most knights do two years in the Academy. You did four, because wards require advanced training in environmental magic and magic theory. The Order invested in you, and they like to get their money's worth, so they would have offered you a 20-year contract, which you must've agreed to since your runes have osmium in them."

He gave me a slow golf clap, wincing. His head still hurt. "Congratulations. You put 2 and 2 together."

"The Order trained you and promised to house and support you for the duration of that 20-year contract, which started when you graduated. The minimum age to enroll in the Order Academy is 18, you finished at 22, and you look to be in your thirties, so you didn't do your deuce."

A hint of life sparked in his sallow eyes, then died down. "That's right."

"They really don't like to kick knight-enchanters out. What was it? Incompetence? Couldn't be, not with the quality of that ward out there. It had to be greed."

"Some people call it greed. I call it proper compensation."

"You would've been paid as a Class V. That's over a hundred grand per year."

He stared at me as if he pitied me. "Is it funny or sad that you think 100K is a decent amount of money? I would figure it out, except I really don't care." He made a *wrap it up* motion with his hand.

"How much did you want?"

"I wanted my due. I gave them all of my twenties. Oh, what a great honor it is to be a knight of the Order of Merciful Aid. So much honor. Such a noble goal. Trudging through shit and blood every day to be wrung dry for the sake of people who won't even thank you, only to finally end up back home, exhausted, and then have to check if you can afford a bottle of Glenfiddich to drown your sorrows."

I held my left thumb and index finger apart a little and made a sawing motion with my right hand.

"Are you playing a tiny violin?" he asked.

"Yep. The name of the song is 'My Heart Bleeds for You.'"

He grimaced. "You're an annoying little fly, aren't you?"

"Yes, but you're still talking to me. How often do you get to talk to someone who understands the Order, Aaron? Tell me, what finally did it?"

"I turned thirty. The night before we'd gone into a sewage treatment plant. There was a small hydra in it, and it threw us around like we were fucking toys. I woke up that morning. My legs hurt. My whole body was black and blue. It hurt to sit up. It hurt to piss. I'd soaked in a tub for an hour the night before, and I could still smell rotting human shit on me. It was in my hair. On my skin. I reeked of it. I looked at myself in the mirror and I decided I was fucking done surviving. It was time to thrive."

"This doesn't look like thriving to me." I indicated the room.

"This came later," he said.

"Ah. Let me guess. You started to moonlight. The Order doesn't like that."

"I was done caring what the Order likes."

"But still, they really don't like to kick knight-enchanters out. You guys are a significant investment for them. They would've ignored your little side jobs."

He snorted. "Little?"

"You must've really fucked up. You warded someone you

shouldn't have warded. The Order came across your ward while pursuing a petition and it must've blown up in their faces. What happened? Did someone die?"

His eyes turned dark. Magic tore out of Aaron and splayed around behind him, like a wave ready to crash down and drown. If it could've made a sound, it would've roared at me like a hurricane.

Wow. Not good. Not good at all.

"Someone did die," I said. "Wow. Sucks to be you."

We stared at each other. The real Aaron was awake now and fully focused on me. Whatever bargain he had made, he'd ended up with a shit-ton of power. He was the magical equivalent of a small nuke.

"Impressive," I said. "But not something you were born with."

He stared at me, his expression harsh.

"Pagan gods come in different flavors," I said. "Some are interested in humans, some are amused by them. And then there is the Tuatha Dé Danann. Everyone knows that of all the gods available, they're the absolute last resort, because they fought us and lost. They didn't assume godhood because of their deeds, they had to assume it to survive. They hate us and everything we stand for."

"Personal experience talking?" Aaron asked. His voice sounded unnaturally deep.

"I've met Morrigan, and I was there when her Hound died, and a new Hound was chosen."

"Mhm. That happened two flares ago. How old were you then? Ten?"

"Don't worry about it," I told him. "Let's talk about that feather over there."

I pointed to the feather above his head.

"That is a swan feather. You've got cold water sponges in your little lab, monsters in your ship, and all sorts of bizarre marine critters having a rave outside. Those cliffs over there, that's probably the coast of Ireland. And then there is the hole itself. There is a nexus of power just through that hole, about twenty or so yards from the ship. That's what's generating all of the magic currents and keeping this gap open. I bet it doesn't close even during tech."

The magic behind Aaron crested.

"Humor me," I said. "I came all this way. Here is what I think happened. You got yourself kicked out of the Order and they blacklisted you by letting everyone know that they would consider anyone who hired you their enemy. Standard procedure. The Knights are not forgiving. So here you were, adrift and abandoned"—thanks, Rimush—"and the Night of the Shining Seas happened. Was it pretty?"

"It was beautiful," he said in his deep, power-saturated voice. "The ocean lit up with blue. The magic was so thick, it made you drunk."

"And in that beautiful moment a deity manifested as a giant swan. You've had a whole semester of Comparative Mythology at the Academy. You know Wilmington's demographics and you knew exactly who that swan was."

"There were four of them," he said. "They were majestic. Breathtaking and glowing with white."

"Four? Well, that's a dead giveaway, isn't it? They must've been unforgettable, the Children of Lyr."

"They were," he said quietly.

"And you trapped one of them in your ward. It must've been a once-in-a-lifetime ward, to catch a god who could both fly and swim. The culmination of all of your training and practice."

Aaron smiled.

"The god couldn't escape and when the eclipse ended and tech came, that majestic swan would die. So you bargained with the father of that god for the life of his child."

"It was Fiachra," he said. "The swan I trapped."

"And his father is Manannán, Lord of the Sea, Guardian of the Otherworld, and Over-King of Tuatha Dé, for whom the Isle of Man is named. That Manannán. That's who you haggled with."

Aaron smiled wider. "Yes."

"What did you ask for?"

"Powers and riches."

"Ah. And here you are, three years later, sitting in this ruin, stealing children and chaining them up. You probably still think you came out on top. You haven't been blessed. You've been cursed, Aaron." I pointed to the kids. "Was it worth it?"

"Yes." His deep voice boomed. "I will get what I am owed."

"On that we agree."

I sprinted toward him, Sarrat in hand.

Aaron clawed the air. The magic wave above him plunged down and turned into real seawater, speeding toward me in a foamy current. Out of the corner of my eye I saw Darin grab Antonio and hold him up above his head.

The wave smashed into me. Like being hit by a charging bull made of concrete. The current jerked me off my feet. I gulped some air, and then the sea swallowed me. The raging water pushed to the back of the room in less than a second. I tried to curl into a ball, but the current was too strong and ice-cold, as if it had come from a melted glacier.

I hit the wall with my left side. Pain shot through my left shoulder all the way down to my fingertips. The impact reverberated through me, and for a second the world dissolved into soft, fuzzy darkness made of agony. The sea gripped me in a watery fist laced with Aaron's magic, squeezing, hurting, threatening to cave my chest in. My bones groaned.

I clawed at the glimmer of the light, holding on to it through the agony, through the pressure, fighting through it, pushing past the threshold of pain. The darkness melted a little. I strained, trying to move my arms. Like trying to lift a car. The water pinned me to the wall, trying to crush me. I couldn't raise my sword. I couldn't even open my eyes. All I managed was a weak twitch.

Aaron's magic burned me through the water. I felt it, a net woven from power borrowed from a god saturating the sea.

My body screamed for air. The memory of Darin lifting the smaller boy up flashed before me. He'd known what was about to happen. This is what Aaron did to them. This is how he punished them.

Not today. Not anymore.

I bit the inside of my mouth. The salty taste of my blood coated my tongue, the magic in it nipping at me with electric sparks.

Air! Air, air, air…

I had almost nothing left in my lungs, and I was about to spend it all.

I choked on my blood. It had to be enough. I strained and spat it out into the current with the most basic of power words. "Hesaad." *Mine.*

The current convulsed like a living creature, a sea serpent caught between my blood and Aaron's net. Seawater roiled, breaking into foam. Waves clashed, its grip on me loosened, and I surfaced long enough to suck in a desperate breath.

The sea pulled me under, and I whispered into it, letting it wash my bloody mouth. Amehe, amehe, amehe…*Obey.*

Something squirmed into my mouth. I tried to bite down on it, but it slipped past my teeth into my throat.

Aaron's net broke. The sea ripped free. My feet touched the bottom, and I kicked up. My head broke the surface. Air. All the sweet air I could ever want.

The water streamed away, and I stood. It was to my armpits and rapidly receding.

My throat was on fire like someone had poured boiling oil into me. My left arm hurt like hell, and when I tried to move my shoulder, it ground, shooting spikes of pain both ways. I couldn't lift it properly.

On the stage Aaron snarled. Magic twisted around him, building again.

I opened my mouth. Nothing came out. No voice. No power.

No matter. I still had my sword.

I started toward Aaron, wading through the water. It was barely to my thighs now, and I was moving fast.

Aaron jerked his hands up. A wallop of magic tore out from his hands and sank into the water in front of him. Three dark knots spun in the sea, sucking up the remaining water until it was barely up my ankle. The nearest whirlpool erupted. A big head broke the water. A round snout, bristling, blue fur, and huge tusks ready to gore.

Manannán's eternal sea swine. Shit.

The whirlpool popped in a fountain of water, and the first pig spilled onto the floor, a walrus-sized monstrosity with porcine front legs armed with 9-inch hooves and tusks the size of carving knives. A forest of bright blue quills rose from its mane. Past its forequarters, the bristles stuck together, transforming into matching scales, and the body flowed seamlessly into a muscular, thick fish tail that coiled behind the beast in a classic Capricorn curve.

The first boar tore across the floor, aiming for me. Two others were forming behind it.

Legend said that Mucca Mhannanain, the eternal swine, provided an endless supply of food to the Tuatha Dé. They continuously regenerated, and the myths were fuzzy on how exactly that happened and how long it took. Killing them permanently was probably impossible. But I didn't have to kill them. I just had to get past them.

The first boar charged, coming at me like a battering ram. Sea, land, it was still a boar, and the club's dance floor was wet and slippery.

The two other boars scrambled across the floor, each on their chosen trajectory.

The first one was almost on me. Wicked tusks gleamed, the unnaturally pale, wet bone reflecting the feylanterns' lights.

I twisted out of the way with zero time to spare, spun, turning, dashed left inches in front of the second boar, sliced at its snout in passing, and threw myself right, out of the third boar's way. The gleaming tusk grazed my thigh in an icy slash, but I kept running.

Behind me the second boar collided with the first and snapped at it, enraged by the bloody gash across its snout. The third boar barreled into them, and they slid across the room in a tangled mass.

Sea hogs weren't made for dancing.

I cleared the room and vaulted onto the stage.

Aaron raised his hands. Gold coins glittered in his fingers. They were large and yellow, with uneven edges, cold struck and minted by hand.

He smiled and hurled two at me. I dodged, but they turned and streaked toward me. One struck my right arm, the other hit my left. Heavy manacles clamped my wrists and sprouted chains that whipped into the water on the floor, where the sea hogs grunted, trying to follow me. The chain jerked my arms straight, sending a bolt of dizzying agony right into my left shoulder. Cold magic swirled through the metal, sinking into my skin.

Aaron held his coins on his palm and flicked them off one by one with his index finger. Two struck my legs and another hit my waist. Manacles clamped around my body. A web of chains shot out from me, sinking into the water. I wasn't going anywhere.

Aaron smiled. "I don't know how you broke out of my net, but I can use you."

Icy water swirled around me in a crystal-clear column and swallowed me whole. It forced its way into me, into my pores, into my nose, my mouth, and began pulling me apart.

"It's very difficult to transform a normal human," Aaron's magic voice echoed in both my ears despite the water filling them. "They don't have enough magic to survive the transformation."

The water pulled on me, trying to reshape me from inside out, and a different version of myself bloomed in my mind, one with gills and a long, glistening tail where my legs used to be.

The sea drew me in. I could feel its currents, sliding just beyond the ship. I heard its song, and it beckoned me. I wanted to swim.

"But you, whoever you are," Aaron whispered. "You have all the magic in the world."

I did. I did have all the magic in the world.

I focused inward, beyond the water, beyond Aaron's magic, to the core of my power. I couldn't speak the words, but I could think them. If faith had power, then thought had magic, and I wouldn't permit my body to be polluted. This was my body, my blood, my bone. I owned it.

I thought the words, sinking all my power into them. *Estene ared dair.*

The magic swelled inside me, thrilled to be unleashed, as if it had been waiting for permission all along. I pushed, directing it to my throat, focusing all of my power on it.

Estene ared dair.

My magic collided with the creature lodged inside me. I strained, pushing hard, harder, through the blinding pain, through the instinctual panic, shaping my magic, wrapping the obstruction in it.

Pushing harder. Harder. Harder…

It came loose. The water around me broke. I gagged and spat out a tiny glowing jellyfish.

The words of a long-forgotten language spilled out on their own, crackling with power.

"ESTENE ARED DAIR." *You have no power over me.*

The chains snapped, fracturing into a thousand pieces, and evaporated. Coins slid off me to the floor.

The old man cringed.

Aaron's mouth gaped open, his face a mask.

"FEAR ME, FOR I AM DEATH WHO COMES TO THE TAKER OF CHILDREN."

The ship quaked, rocked by the language of power. The sea hogs screamed in panic.

"ARRAT NASU SAR OR."

Magic jerked Aaron off his feet, into the air, pulling his legs and arms taut.

"ARRAT UR AHU KARSARAN."

His arms snapped, bones breaking in too many places to count. Aaron screamed. His magic splashed around him, broiling, but it couldn't counter mine.

"ARRAT UR PIRID KARSARAN."

His leg bones fractured. It sounded like firecrackers.

"OHIR GAMAR."

The human bag of shattered bones who used to be Aaron landed on the stage. He howled as I walked to him, as I raised my sword, and as I struck, until Sarrat's blade finally cut off his scream.

The sea swine melted back into seawater. The ocean streamed back through the gap in the hull, leaving puddles in its stead.

I raised Aaron's head by its hair and turned to the old man.

He fell to his knees and smashed his forehead onto the stage with a thud.

My voice was hoarse. "Anyone else here who thinks he is a god?"

His voice quaked. "No, mistress."

"Good."

I turned to the nine prisoners.

The chains on their ankles had not disappeared. Damn.

"Darin?" I called.

He looked at me, startled.

"I'm a friend of your father."

Darin blinked at me, clearly shocked. "My dad?"

"Yes. Thomas. I need you to explain what went on here."

THE CHEST OF GOLD SAT ON THE SEA FLOOR, ABOUT 20 FEET down. The water was crystal-clear, and from my spot on the edge of the hull's hole, every detail of it was visible. The dumpster-sized wooden box rested among the coral-textured boulders, encrusted with sea stars and urchins. Its carved lid was flung open, showing the gleaming treasure inside—a mound of gold coins, bright yellow like egg yolks, heaped in a small mountain and punctuated by glowing jewels. A god's ransom. Literally.

Aaron had asked Manannán for powers and riches. He'd shown me his powers. That chest was the promised riches.

"On their first dive, everyone gets a coin," Darin said. "Just one. The moment you touch the gold, you get chained up."

Their chains led to that chest, growing from it like roots.

"Once you get that first coin and get chained, you bring it to Aaron, and he sends you back for more. Except you can dive all you want, and it won't matter. You can touch the chest, you can scoop the coins up, but when you try to take them out of the water, they disappear."

"And Aaron didn't get chained when he touched those first coins?" I asked.

"Once you get a coin out of the water, anyone can hold it," Darin said. "But only Aaron could use them."

So each of Aaron's coins came from that chest and cost the freedom of the diver. He didn't dive for the coins himself. Otherwise, he would've been bound like the rest of them. No, he must've suspected that Manannán's ransom came with a catch. He must've hired some kind of mer-person to fetch them, and once they got ensnared by the chest, he started kidnapping people.

Each of those coins radiated magic, and it was strong. The more coins, the stronger Aaron's powers became.

"He would make us dive all the time," the younger woman said.

"Hours and hours. Even though we couldn't bring anything back, he kept sending us in."

The treasure really didn't want me to ignore it. I wanted to keep looking at it. I wanted to dive down and touch those shiny yellow coins. To feel the metal rub against the ridges of my fingertips.

Aaron would've stared at it just like this. He could see it, but he couldn't touch it. Three years of staring. It must've slowly driven him mad.

"Aaron stood right here often, didn't he?" I asked.

"He'd stare at it for hours," the woman with defiant eyes said. "Watching us as we swam back and forth, trying to bring the gold to him. Bastard."

I was right. Manannán had cursed Aaron for daring to put his hands on his child, and he'd used gold to do it. It wasn't surprising. He'd done it before. One time he had tempted Cormac mac Airt, the High King of Ireland, with a silver branch that bore three gold apples, and Cormac had become so obsessed with it that he had given Manannán his daughter, his son, and his wife just to possess it.

It was a hell of a trap. Manannán must've ripped a tear in the fabric of the world, connecting this spot to his coast where his powers were the strongest. He had dropped this chest on his side of the portal, fully within his power and in his domain, and then he had told Aaron to go get his treasure.

The golden hoard glittered. This was the source of the magic that was keeping the portal open. And every time anyone looked at it, Manannán got a little boost of power.

Because people didn't just look at it—they coveted it.

Aaron had wanted to possess it, the captives had wanted to carry it so they could earn their freedom, and all of them had unwittingly worshipped Manannán every time they had swum to it. His own faith generator.

This wasn't just devious. It was Machiavellian.

He would not want to give it up.

"Can't you break it?" The defiant woman showed me her chain.

I shook my head.

"But I saw you. We all saw you…"

"Aaron was right. I have a lot of magic," I said. "I'm very difficult to restrain. Tuatha Dé are cunning and malicious. Nothing they do is ever simple. Cutting through the chains is an obvious solution, and Manannán would've accounted for it. If I try to sever your chains, it might kill you."

Her face twisted.

"So what do we do?" the other woman asked.

It took a bit of effort to turn away from the treasure.

I walked back to the stage and jumped onto it. Five gold coins lay glistening on the floor, where they had fallen when I broke my chains. Five coins but nine divers.

I looked at the old man, still kneeling with his forehead planted on the floor tiles. He hadn't moved.

"You."

"Garvey is here!" he proclaimed.

"Bring me the rest of the coins. All of them. I've already cut off two heads today. Don't force me to make it three."

He climbed to his feet and rushed off.

I went back to Aaron's body, pulled out my knife, and cut a chunk off his robe, the one with the pocket on it. Using my knife, I nudged the coins into the pocket. I didn't want to touch them.

The old man returned, huffing, and set a small wooden chest in front of me. I opened it. Seven more coins lying on blue velvet. I turned to the prisoners. "There are nine of you."

"Kostya, Chandi, and Ari didn't make it," the younger woman said. "Aaron raged out sometimes."

I had to get them free. No matter what it cost.

I emptied the pocket into the chest and handed it to Darin. "Take this down and put them back."

He leaped into the water, cutting into it without a splash, and streaked to the treasure chest. Didn't change shape. Like father, like son. Cautious.

"Will this fix it?" the angry woman demanded.

"Probably not, but it's a good first step."

The coins tumbled out of the small chest into the big one. The chains remained.

It would've been too simple.

Darin swam back and climbed up to stand next to me. "What now?"

I looked at Antonio, the little boy without a chain. "Are there any more kids like you? Without chains?"

He shook his head.

"Any other people who are here against their will?"

"Leslie."

"Who is Leslie?"

"She is a cook," Antonio said.

"Okay. Go get Leslie and have her bring whatever fuel she has in the kitchen. Oil, spirits, anything like that. And then you, and Leslie, and Garvey can help me gather wood. We're going to build a bonfire, and then we're going to pray."

EITHER THE CRUISE SHIP HADN'T BOTHERED WITH FLAME RETARDANT upholstery, or the magic somehow canceled it out, because the tower of chairs we'd gathered into a big pile went up like candles. We'd doused them in cooking oil and kerosene from the kitchen, but we might've as well not bothered. They burned like tinder despite the damp.

Hopefully the ceiling wouldn't cave in on us.

We hadn't found any more disciples while gathering wood. I had sent Antonio to all the places where they gathered, but he found only empty chairs. The woman who'd led me down to the arch must've gotten everyone off the ship. As far as I was concerned, letting them leave was more mercy than they deserved. If someone remained, it was on them.

"I'm not praying to him!" Elaine clenched her fists, making the scars on her arms stand out. "He's the reason I'm here. Ten months! Ten months I haven't seen my baby. My husband probably thinks I'm dead. My parents..."

Solina, the younger chained-up woman, hugged her.

Of all of them, Elaine had the most fight left in her, but she was like a knife that had been sharpened too much—dangerous yet brittle. She'd almost attacked the old man. Garvey had served Aaron voluntarily. He hadn't been a slave or taken against his will; he had witnessed everything Aaron had done, and he'd stayed because Aaron had made it worth his while. Garvey deserved everything she wanted to do to him, but Elaine didn't deserve having to live with it.

"I know it's hard," I told her. "And you're angry. You have a right to be angry. But we must get these chains off so everyone can go home. If you won't do it for yourself, do it for the kids."

Elaine looked around at the clump of chained-up children. Her expression went slack.

"Are we good?" I asked her.

She nodded.

I pulled a small plastic bag out of one of my belt pockets and emptied the mix of herbs into the fire. Blue sparks burst from the fire, filling the air with a thick, smoky aroma. I funneled my magic into the flames, pulled a small vial of my blood out of another pocket, and dripped a few drops into the bonfire.

The flames turned crimson.

The fire pulsed with magic like a giant heart beating.

I didn't even try to speak Gaelic. I only knew a handful of words, and I'd offend him more than anything. He'd bargained with Aaron so he'd understand me.

"Manannán mac Lir," I said, sending another splash of magic

into the fire.

"Manannán mac Lir," the chained people intoned behind me.

"Son of the Sea."

"Son of the Sea."

"Lord of Emain Ablach…"

"Lord of Emain Ablach…"

"Mag Mell, and Tír Tairngire." Some of those were technically synonymous, but no god ever wanted less titles. I kept going, echoed by a chorus.

"Over-King of Tuatha Dé Danann, Weaver of Magic Mists Féth Fíada, He who Captains the Self-Guiding Boat Sguaba Tuinne, He who Rides the Steed Aonbharr, your people seek you in their hour of need. We beg you to speak to us."

They were his people. They might have come from different mythological origins, but all of them were people of the sea.

Nothing. Just ruby-colored flames. I hadn't expected him to answer right away. It was a very long shot. Most deities refused to manifest, even for the briefest instant. Not only that, but this entire set-up functioned as a faith factory for him. That dumpster of gold was proof of his existence and power. He would know that I was calling to end it, and he'd be reluctant to part with it.

I didn't share that fact with anyone because Elaine was on edge as it was. I needed them united and committed to begging.

The fire crackled.

I started over. "Manannán mac Lir, Son of the Sea…"

Fire calls were like a ringing phone, annoying and difficult to ignore. And I had a feeling Manannán might have gotten himself an avatar. In the myths, he liked to travel. The fire call would bug him even more than usual.

"Manannán mac Lir, Son of the Sea…"

"Manannán mac Lir, Son of the Sea…"

"Manannán mac Lir, Son of the Sea…"

"Manannán mac Lir, Son of the Sea…"

The flames flashed blue. A man rose from the fire. Tall, broad-shouldered, and muscular, he was naked to the waist. A long kilt or a belted robe hung off his hips, merging with the flames. His long hair and beard were the color of sea foam. His eyes were a deep, piercing blue.

"What?" Manannán demanded.

Finally.

I knelt. Everyone behind me knelt as well.

"Aaron is dead. We've returned your gold. Please release your people from your chains."

"Who are you to bargain with me?"

"The killer of Neig."

The deity pondered me. I kept kneeling. Dropping a dragon's name should buy me some street cred.

"I meant for him to suffer for eternity. You've cut it short. You released him from his penance."

"He was wrong to ransom your child. But since then, he has taken other children from their families. They suffer the way your child suffered, separated from their parents, denied the warmth and love of their family. They are innocent. We beg you to undo these chains."

"They should be punished with him. All of you should be punished for allowing him to live and harm my child."

I was wrong for killing him and also wrong for allowing him to live, and everyone should suffer. Tuatha Dé, ever so consistent and reasonable.

"We've corrected our mistake."

"Too little, too late."

I made a small motion with my hand. The three smallest children crawled forward, crying and wailing. We'd rehearsed it.

"Please, Father of Fiachra, Father of Niamh…"

The kids cried.

"…Father of Eachdond Mor, Father of…"

He grunted. **"Enough! What do you offer?"**

Shit. He wanted an offering. I didn't have anything. Nothing valuable enough.

Think, think, think...

"What do you offer in compensation?" Manannán repeated.

"This ship."

"This ruin?"

"This ship is a monument to human arrogance. It had cost untold riches to build and been filled with luxurious treasures, and yet it wasn't used to transport goods or carry people across the waves from one destination to another. It went around in a circle, returning to the same port with all of its passengers still on board. It was built specifically for leisure, so humanity, in its conceit, could spend a few days floating on the ocean and scoffing at its power. It's the vessel of people who thought they had conquered the sea."

Manannán considered it. I held my breath.

"Is it yours to give?"

"Yes. I killed Aaron, so everything that was his is now ours. Please accept this vessel as our humble offering."

"I agree. Remember my mercy."

"Always, Lord Manannán."

He disappeared.

The chains fractured and vanished. Someone cried out, as if unable to believe it.

The sea surged through the hole, licked the fire, and put it out in an instant.

Far ahead, at the cliffs, a wall of water rose, dark and menacing, climbing higher and higher. Something moved inside it. Something with very long tentacles.

"We have to go!" I barked.

Solina grabbed Antonio's hand. "This way!"

Everyone ran after her, and I brought up the rear, keeping the kids in front of me. Garvey followed us, scrambling to keep up. We dashed down the pitch-black hallway, scurrying through the bowels of the ship on feel alone.

Elaine made a sharp right turn ahead. The caravan of kids followed her and so did I. Mark, the gaunt man, scooped the smallest child up and carried her.

Something hit the hull. The colossal ship trembled.

Boom!

Boom! Boom!

My brain helpfully supplied a vision of enormous tentacles wrapping around the vessel.

I burst through the door after the kids, into a stairwell dimly lit by a single feylantern above. The children pounded up the metal stairs. I rushed upward. One turn. Two…

The door behind me burst open. Garvey hauled his bony body through it and started up the stairs.

Round and round, we charged up the stairs.

The door below us snapped open again. Water shot into the stairwell, foaming and rising.

"Faster!" I yelled.

The kids huffed in front of me, slowing down.

The water caught Garvey. A long, buttery creature swirled in its depths, wrapped around the old man, and pulled him under.

The ship groaned, metal screeching, and *moved*.

I clung to the stairs.

The ship froze again.

"Almost there!" Solina screamed.

The kids stomped up the steps. I chased them.

Ahead a door banged open.

I rounded the stairs and burst through the door onto a deck fifty feet above the sea. I was on the side facing the shore. The beach was a thousand feet away. A gigantic octopus tentacle, ten feet across, gripped the ship next to me.

When that monstrosity pulled the ship into Manannán's domain, it would take us with it. Even if we jumped down into the sea, when the ship moved, it would generate a current that would suck us in, and Manannán wouldn't let us go.

We had to make it to solid ground before he took the ship. That was our only hope.

The children leaped off the deck into the water below.

The tentacles squeezed. Metal screamed in protest.

A thousand feet to the shore. And so far down.

Darin grabbed my hand and ran to the deck. I didn't have time to think about it. The deck ended, the water yawned at me, for a terrified moment I was airborne, and then I plunged into the ocean.

The water swallowed me. I went in deep and kicked randomly, not sure which way was up. In front of me, the dark mass of the cruise ship slid backward, dragged off by something too colossal for a human mind to comprehend. A current gripped me, pulling me back toward the ship.

Darin shifted. His body twisted, and then the human was gone. A merman looked at me with turquoise eyes, his body flowing into a powerful fish tail. Darin spun me around, and we shot away from the Emerald Wave as if dragged by a speed boat.

The sea gripped us, not wanting to let go, trying to pull us back toward the cruise ship.

Darin sped up.

We flew through the ocean depth, trying to fight against the current.

There wasn't enough air.

Suddenly the pressure vanished. Darin stopped and pulled me up. We surfaced. The sandy beach was only twenty feet away. I dropped my feet and touched the bottom.

The sky above us glowed gently with the promise of sunrise, pink and lavender brightening the deep indigo of the retreating night. The Emerald Wave was gone, and the strange nexus of magic had vanished with it.

I took a deep breath and lay on my back. I was so tired.

Something splashed through the water toward me, but I was too exhausted to react.

Curran's face appeared above me. "Hey, baby."

I reached out and touched his face. Real and warm. "Hey."

"Went swimming without me?"

"I thought you might catch up."

He wrapped his arms around me. "I was delayed."

"They showed up?"

"They did."

The first sliver of sun broke the horizon. The water sparkled. A couple dozen feet away, Antonio and Leslie staggered onto the beach, holding hands. A tan, naked man with red hair paced up and down the surf, looking nervously in our direction.

"Is our son okay?"

"Yes."

"Are you okay?"

"Yes."

"Good." I snuggled against him. "Who is the naked guy on the beach?"

"Troy. He's a medmage. He says he trained with Doolittle."

"Oh good. I think my left arm is broken."

Curran made a low growling noise. I put my good arm around him and kissed him.

A beautiful mermaid slid past us in the water, her dark, curly hair streaming behind her in wet spirals, her eyes bright red, and I realized it was Solina. She was smiling.

"Ready to go home?" Curran asked.

"In a minute."

In the distance Darin leaped out of the water, his tail a brilliant, heart-breaking blue. Behind him the rest of the kids jumped like a pod of dolphins, their tails, fins, and scales glistening.

We floated in the warm water, while the sun rose and the merchildren from a dozen myths played in the waves.

THE END

ACKNOWLEDGMENTS

All the thanks in the world to

Nancy Yost and the lovely team at NYLA for dropping everything and working on this story on super short notice;

Rossana Sasso for the content edit;

Stefanie Chin for the copyedit;

Maura O'Toole, Maria Rumorh, Harriet Chow, Katherine Heasley, Cassandra Bell, and Gail Leifkovitz for the beta edit;

and Jeaniene Frost for hysterically laughing when we told her this was going to be a "short story."

ALSO BY ILONA ANDREWS

Kate Daniels World

BLOOD HEIR

Kate Daniels Series

MAGIC BITES

MAGIC BLEEDS

MAGIC BURNS

MAGIC STRIKES

MAGIC MOURNS

MAGIC BLEEDS

MAGIC DREAMS

MAGIC SLAYS

GUNMETAL MAGIC

MAGIC GIFTS

MAGIC RISES

MAGIC BREAKS

MAGIC STEALS

MAGIC SHIFTS

MAGIC STARS

MAGIC BINDS

MAGIC TRIUMPHS

The Iron Covenant

IRON AND MAGIC

UNTITLED IRON AND MAGIC #2

Hidden Legacy Series

BURN FOR ME

WHITE HOT

WILDFIRE

DIAMOND FIRE

SAPPHIRE FLAMES

EMERALD BLAZE

RUBY FEVER

Innkeeper Chronicles Series

CLEAN SWEEP

SWEEP IN PEACE

ONE FELL SWEEP

SWEEP OF THE BLADE

SWEEP WITH ME

SWEEP OF THE HEART

Kinsmen

SILENT BLADE

SILVER SHARK

THE KINSMEN UNIVERSE (anthology with both SILENT BLADE and SILVER SHARK)

FATED BLADES

The Edge Series

ON THE EDGE

BAYOU MOON

FATE'S EDGE

STEEL'S EDGE

ABOUT THE AUTHOR

Ilona Andrews is the pseudonym for a husband-and-wife writing team, Gordon and Ilona. They currently reside in Texas with their two children and numerous dogs and cats. The couple are the #1 *New York Times* and *USA Today* bestselling authors of the Kate Daniels and Kate Daniels World novels as well as The Edge and Hidden Legacy series. They also write the Innkeeper Chronicles series, which they post as a free weekly serial.

For a complete list of their books, fun extras, and Innkeeper installments, please visit their website www.ilona-andrews.com.

CPSIA information can be obtained
at www.ICGtesting.com
Printed in the USA
LVHW031638020223
738518LV00007B/428

9 781641 972529

7